RANGER'S WISH

A TEXAN DEVILS
CHRISTMAS NOVELLA

SOFIA AVES

First published in All I Want for Christmas anthology, Romance Collections, 2020

Published by Little Quail Press

Cover Art by JS Designs Cover Art

Editing Services provided by A. Strom - Edits with a Coffee Addict

www.redpensandcoffeebeans.wordpress.com/
www.facebook.com/redpensandcoffeebeans/

ISBN 978-1-922448-12-5

III

Published by Little Quail Press

ISBN 978-1-922448-12-5

CONTENTS

CONTENTS

DEDICATION

Jacinta & Courtney,
thanks for reminding me Texas Rangers are
real.

Andy Matthews is a third-generation Texas Ranger.
Known locally as the Texan Devils,
Andy has always been one of the *good* guys.

But this Christmas, his loyalties will be tested...

CHAPTER ONE

ANDY

Fake badges scattered the surface of my desk, setting it aglow beneath the string of Christmas lights our secretary had strung across the entire office. I pushed them aside with one hand, where they dribbled to the industrial carpet in a merry cascade.

"Why are we doing this again? You can't tell me a Ranger's time is best taken up with small-time forgeries." I looked around the office, blinking beneath the festiveness overpopulating our workplace.

Tinsel and fairy lights dangled from the ceiling, and a haphazard bunch of mistletoe was pinned to the top of the door frame.

That was new. Was it supposed to look like that? I closed one eye and tilted my head. Yeah, much better. My vision blurred. I swiped a calloused and cracked hand over tired eyes. My boss had shot off on a personal vendetta, leaving me in charge of the team for the festive season — our busiest time of year.

And while I didn't *not* appreciate the vote of confidence, stretching myself across too many minor jobs to assist local law enforcement took my eye off my actual purpose. Anything darker that might be brewing could be too easily overlooked at this time of year. Which really, was how we had gotten ourselves to this point as it was.

Sam Bernie's empty desk had become the elephant in the room. Pristine and shining, it was nothing like how it had appeared while the Major was alive. He'd been shot outside his house only a week before, the shooter crossing state lines.

My boss had launched after him, regardless that it was well outside of our jurisdiction, unable to wait for the local uniforms to get their act together to serve justice. But Archer had his own particular brand of vengeance in mind, and no one could stop him when he set out to finish something.

A sharp something bit into my palm and I bit back a yelp. Straightening my fingers, I studied the badge indented into my hand. The thing might be fake as hell, but it still packed a bite.

I was so engrossed in the random thoughts flitting around my head that I missed the extra body entering the office.

Jake thumped my desktop, the remaining badges on it jingling with a tinny sound.

This is what I get for being distracted.

I winced. "You've been talking at me for a while, right?" I yawned, leaning back to stretch cramped muscles. God, I was tight. Driving a desk had never been my style of law enforcement. I needed to go to the gym, somewhere warm and covered — jogging in blisteringly cold conditions was not my idea of fun.

"Yeah, but it's not like you usually listen to me, so..." Jake trailed off, grinning. White blond hair flopped into his face, though he made no move to push it back. His black leather jacket wasn't regulation either, but that was typical Jake, The cheeky Ranger pushed the boundaries with every step. And so long as he did his job well, he knew he could scrape in with getting away with it.

I shook my head, the effort required to sass him too much. He ducked the fake badge I tossed at him.

"Get outta here. Don't you have some family celebration to get to?"

"Nope." His grin widened.

I shook my head. "Girlfriend? There *was* one of those...right?"

Jake's grin turned sour. "Yeah. But... Well. Let's just say I'm at a loose end for this year, huh?" His eyes flared with a slightly manic look to them, and in lieu of keeping my own sanity, I decided not to go there.

"Well, uh, that sucks, hey? I need to wake myself up. Gonna take the stairs to get a coffee. You want one?"

"Nah, it'll be cold by the time you get up here if you take the stairs, old man."

"Don't you *old man* me." I rose too fast after too many hours in the chair, and tossed a half-hearted punch at his shoulder that he dodged easily. "You're a damned year older than me."

I left him grumbling in the office, grabbing my jacket as I jogged the few flights to the ground floor. By the time I hit the street, I was already half-frozen. The lack of real work had me tossing around the idea of jamming my nose into some of the local cop's jurisdiction, but that would only cause my bosses grief when they got back — whenever that was likely to be.

4

Thankfully, police shootings were down — a rarity at this time of year, but I was glad the tragedies had ceased for the main part. Not wanting to get myself in strife with my bosses or step on any toes, my thoughts turned to the small Ranger-related crimes I was currently working. But before I made it too far, the icy air that used the street front as its own personal wind tunnel wiped my mind blank.

Though the sky was clear, the wind had a chill factor that promised an icy — if not a white — Christmas.

Our local coffee shop was right across the street from the office. I was sure they survived on our orders alone. Calling it in for a delivery when their line died down might have been easier, but my body badly needed extra movement.

I grabbed an extra cup for Jake regardless of his objections — he'd whine at me for the afternoon shift if I didn't — and jogged back across the road, my pale shadow long beneath the weak afternoon sunlight.

Stacking my cups one atop the other, I grabbed the handle for the stairwell. It stuck. I jiggled it for a moment,

5

comprehension finally hitting me as it gave, drawing inwards, and lurching me with it.

I found myself the sudden bearer of an armload of garlands and tinsel. Holly poked me in the face and a pine needle worked its way up one nostril. I resisted the urge to sneeze, shifting slightly to remove the offensive tree in my face.

Peering into the mass to make sure my coffee tower had survived, I spotted a suspiciously familiar auburn head.

"Ella?"

"MMpphwh fffsssk there."

I grinned. Definitely Ella. "What was that?"

"Mmmphh said—" Her head broke through the clutter of pine needles in my arms, bright eyes meeting mine. I had the pleasure of watching them widen, before the familiar scent of her overrode the forest in my arms. My body reacted to her instantly, my jeans far too tight for comfort. "Andy?" Her mouth hung open, unable to disguise the pink tip of her nose that always came out when she was flustered.

Hazel eyes caught mine and held them.

Still the same Ella as always. My first and always.

6

"Yeah." My mouth dried. I swallowed, but words deserted me.

Ella appeared to be suffering in a similar vein.

"Um. Merry Christmas?" she tried, still staring. Ella bit her bottom lip, and I knew she was holding back whatever wanted to blurt from her rose-red mouth.

"Merry Christmas," I murmured, my eyes locked on her lip where it slid between her teeth, slightly swollen. I dragged my eyes back to her face before I did something highly inappropriate in the lobby of Ranger Headquarters. "Do you want to, uh—" I wiggled my shoulders, not game to release anything in case I dropped the lot.

"Oh! Um. I'm just going to—" Ella's head sank out of my line of sight, dropping out from the bottom of the knot of garlands.

Pine needles tickled my nose a second time as a vision of her on her knees before me had my cock twitching until I was painfully hard.

Her fine hands brushed my stomach, doing nothing for my current state as she removed the forest from my arms. I remembered to clutch the coffees in time to prevent her from wearing them.

7

Propping her chin on top of the green mass, she gave me a smile that lit my world. Her hair tumbled in waves over the top of everything, thick lashes framing eyes I had lost myself in too often to count, though that had been years ago. Something twitched again, and it took me a moment to realize it was my heart, this time.

"Um. You wanna move, Ranger?" Her head cocked to the side, and I recalled where we were.

And that I was staring at her with a dumb smile on my face, the way I had when I was in high school. But I wasn't sixteen anymore.

"Oh. Of course." I stepped aside, pinning the door back with my boot.

She sent a quick grin over her shoulder and hurtled out the front doors to the building. Dressed in her typical blue jeans and a filmy top, she looked almost exactly as she had the last time I'd seen her, even wearing a pair of tan boots I could swear were the same as the ones I'd bought for her birthday before we parted company.

"Hold it, would you? I'll be back in a minute!" She shot around the corner, out of my line of sight.

I leaned against the door and finally took a sip of coffee. It was lukewarm. Jake wouldn't be too pleased, but the other Ranger's preferences were reasonably low on my list for the time being.

"Don't you have anything better to do?" A hand tapped me on my shoulder. I choked on my coffee, barely avoiding spilling the lot down my front. "Reactions aren't what they're meant to be, Matthews."

I whipped my head around, catching sight of Christian Henderson, dressed in his customary white shirt and silver lariat. Everything else was black — his hair, hat, jeans, boots. It was like looking at a black void in a world of color.

"Don't you do something that requires more brawn than brains? Why are you here, Henderson?" I eyed the Ranger with open dislike.

"Looking for your boss. Either one of them will do." Hands jammed in jeans too tight for his skinny legs, he looked around in an obvious fashion.

I rolled my eyes. "You won't find him here. He's ah– off. On vacation. For Christmas."

Resisting the urge to cuss myself, I closed my mouth instead, nipping my tongue

9

with my teeth. Could I have fumbled that any worse? Maybe the Silly Season had gone to my head.

Maybe it was seeing Ella again.

"Hmm. On vacation...hunting a certain murderer?" Henderson looked me straight in the eyes. I'd get ripped a new one for letting that out. "Not your fault." He clapped me on the shoulder again. I gritted my teeth at the unwelcome contact. "It was an easy guess."

I narrowed my eyes; the way he strung out *guess* in his customary and put-on twang made me think it hadn't been my fault at all. Everything appeared to be fake today.

A hint of honeysuckle and pine needles brushed over me.

There's nothing fake in that.

Henderson stepped back as Ella bustled back through the front doors, making a beeline straight for me. Arms full of wreaths, she called out a muffled *thanks* and tore up the stairwell, taking the stairs a jaunty two steps at a time. Her jeans hid nothing of the curves of hips and an ass that I could have watched all day. Would she be just another, short-lived interlude in my work day? Each blended into the next, with her a light amongst the blur. My chest

10

clenched at the thought of seeing her so briefly.

I turned back to Henderson, inhaling a controlled breath. "Have a merry— whatever." I tapped my heel on the fire escape door, letting it begin to swing shut behind me.

"Not a bad distraction you have there," Henderson called after me.

I gritted my teeth, mindful of my tongue this time, and refused to rise to his bait. The stairs gave me a reason for my elevated heart rate, though I didn't puff as I pounded the concrete in her wake, catching up with her on the second flight without spilling coffee all over myself.

Admiring her toned figure in her trademark skinny jeans, caramel boots, and loose, flowy top, I reflected wryly that Henderson had been right. Ella was a distraction.

A very welcome one.

CHAPTER TWO

ELLA

The stairwell rang with a second set of footsteps. I breathed hard, torn between wanting to race up the rest of the stairs before he could catch up to me or slowing down so I could spend more time with him. The feel of him so close army body reacting in ways I hadn't for so long, and the heat that always seemed to roll off that incredible chest and shoulders had me wishing the garlands hadn't been between us at all.

I shook my head, attempting to clear it, but he had always hit the sweet spot for me, and my head — or my heart — seemed intent on reminding me of that. Gripping the garlands firmly, but not tight enough to crush them, I attempted to clear my head.

Taking the stairs faster with my balancing skills would likely end with me face planting on the stairwell with Christmas wreaths raining down on any unfortunate souls below. And then he'd rescue me, the same as he always had.

Him being Andy Matthews. Career Texas Ranger — excuse me, *Texan Devil*, as they were locally known — who'd spent years working his way through the ranks to where he was now as part of the special ops unit in Austin and an all-around nice guy.

Not that I'd been stalking him at all. My cheeks heated at the thought, and I pretended to convince myself that I needed to be fitter. Which was an Andy-sized lie I couldn't get away from. When I'd been contracted to supply displays for the building, I'd had to check if he was housed there. And of course, he was. I'd managed to get through my first two days of decorating without running into him, but my chances had run through, it seemed.

He was also my first love.

Which made him my ex-boyfriend. The two just wouldn't go together, no matter how hard I tried. It sounded stupid even in my head; there was no chance I was saying that aloud.

There'd been two broken hearts at the end of that short-lived relationship. Short but intense, dating Andy Matthews was unlike dating anyone else, especially for a sixteen-year-old girl who had stars in her eyes when a senior asked her out.

14

I kept repeating that same lie to myself and I pushed my way up the stairs, trying not to remember the feel of his hands on my skin, how the weight of him pressed me into the bed, the heat from his skin— I swallowed hard, my face flaming hotter than ever.

Unfit, you're utterly unfit.

Liar, liar. Though I'd likely boast sore calves after the several trips I'd done on the stairs already, delivering Christmas arrangements.

"Ella. Wait," Andy caught up with me far too fast, his long legs making the trip much easier for him. He stopped on the step below me, bringing him down to almost my own height as I turned to face him. Almost. At six feet and two inches, Andy was usually one of the tallest guys in the room.

"Hey, Andy." I considered hiding behind a bunch of poinsettias, then decided that was too cowardly, even for me. I'd done enough running away.

"Can I help with anything?"

I peered over the top of everything, spotting the two takeaway cups he clutched. "You have your hands full, but..." Ever helpful, Andy would be crushed if I knocked back his offer. I scouted about for a reason he could use. "Um, you could grab this door for me, please?" I nodded to the stairwell door at the landing just above me.

"Got it." He squeezed past me, his knuckles brushing my waist where he held his coffees in a death grip. He grinned, sending my heart off on a sprint again.

Dammit.

"Thanks," I croaked.

The familiar scent of soap and leather wafted under my nose, bringing more memories to the forefront of my mind that I couldn't deal with just now.

"Ella?"

I looked up to find Andy holding the door open, his eyes alight with curiosity. Or maybe it was memory, too. I was surprised he'd even speak to me after what I'd done, but then, he'd always been the nice guy.

"Thanks," I mumbled again, edging past him. I popped out of the doorway, stumbling over my own feet. The grace department had clearly missed me whenever it was passed around.

Warm hands slid around my waist, steadying me. Andy straightened me, his fingers lingering at the edges of my top. "You okay?"

Was it so terrible to want to feel his hands on my skin? I nodded, not trusting myself to speak. Certainly not enough to turn around to face him, when he was so close.

How can he possibly affect me like this after ten years?

I shook my head, forcing a laugh at my own expense. "You know me, still a massive clutz."

Determined to finish my job without hindering anyone else — or myself, I took a step forward, pretending I wasn't disappointed when the contact with him was broken.

"I do know you," he said, still far too close behind me, the deep timbre of his voice sending a thrill over me. I clung to my poinsettia bundled between an armful of wreaths. "Are those for up here?"

He gestured to my arms, plucking the top wreath from the pile. It had been the capstone of my creation, and without it, the bundle in my arms began to fall apart.

I grabbed for them all at once, wreaths slipping from my grasp in haphazard directions. "Grab that one!" I called as one wreath took many with it in a cascade of green and red.

Floundering, Andy reached for the lot, bumping straight into me. I landed on my rump, admitting ruefully that perhaps I wasn't as fit as I had thought, the extra padding having served me well.

"Oh, Ella. I'm so sorry." Andy liberated the remaining wreaths from me, placing them carefully on a nearby desk.

I gathered the few on the floor, noting they were still in mostly good condition, though one was fairly squashed. The poinsettia alone appeared to have survived unscathed. I placed it on the nearest desk for safe keeping, and returned to assess the remaining decorations. Pinecones tangled amongst red velvet ribbons and fir branches. I picked a few strands apart; some had survived, and I could use them to fix any of the others that had minor damage.

For the second time, Andy's hands closed around me, setting me back on my feet. Sapphire eyes contemplated me, though his mouth turned up in a wide smile.

"Thank you," I muttered to the carpet, breaking away from his gaze. I swallowed, unwilling to be drawn into him, no matter how much I wanted to.

He has a career and a life.

Yes, thank you, brain. We've been here before.

"It's okay. You need help with putting these...uh, where were you putting them?"

I withdrew an order slip from my back pocket, glad to have a reason not to look at him. "Three down the hall, one downstairs — I was going to do that one on my way out — and...five for in here."

Ticking my list off in my head, I waved vaguely at the room under the pretense of folding the piece of paper into a tiny square and stuffing it back into my jeans. Silence fell between us as I stared at the shiny toes of his boots, resisting the urge to hide my very old and very scuffed ones.

Finally, I gave in to the urge and looked up.

Andy grinned at me, his deep azure eyes contagious in their sparkling humor.

I grinned back. "What?"

"You really are still you, aren't you?" Andy swept his hand over his own wavy hair, which looked like he'd just stepped out of a barber. Or maybe a magazine.

"Same." I watched his movements, mesmerised by grace he had never seemed to notice he had. Not in how his shoulders sloped in a relaxed fashion, but still held

19

pride in his job and himself, or how his hand rested comfortably on his belt. No ring, I noted. *Stalker.* "I mean, I'm the same. Nothing's changed." I winced, closing my mouth firmly.

"Yeah," Andy said, not exactly laughing at me, but coming close to it. His eyes sparkled at me as he returned to the issue at hand. "So five of these, uh, things. In here. Going where?" His forehead dipped as his gaze flicked about the office with no small degree of panic.

I turned around, hiding a smile. Andy never had been very good at hiding his emotions. It was one of the traits of being such an honest man. Just another thing I had always loved about him. I began to point out a few places the decorations would fit, coming full circle around the office and back to face Andy. The smile had faded from his face, replaced with a question.

"What?"

He shook his head. "This is what you do now?"

I raised an eyebrow. "Yes. I have a small florist shop in Cedar Park. It's just a work from home type business. It's a very small thing."

20

I dropped my gaze to study the carpet again, willing myself to disappear. Here I was, standing in front of an ex-boyfriend who had made an amazing career from what he loved doing, while I fessed up to playing with flowers all day long.

"It sounds good," Andy said, sounding wistful.

I raised my head in disbelief, but there was no lie written on his face. His reputation as an honest man had helped with his application into the Rangers. Some small part of me loved that nothing crucial about him had changed, that my favorite parts were still there. That, and those shoulders.

"It's very small." I picked up the squashed wreath, plucking more strands free and eyeing the others which needed repair. "I'll fix these up and get out of your hair."

"No, honestly, it's no worry—" Andy cut himself off as one of the coffees was snatched from his hands by another Ranger who downed the thing in a massive gulp. He swallowed it, turning purple. I discreetly stepped out of firing range in case he failed, Andy's face reddening in a tell-tale trait as he struggled to hold back a laugh.

"That's ice-cold," the Ranger gasped, managing to get it all down without spraying

21

the room. "What the hell, Andy? Sorry, Ma'am." He gave me a nod, then turned back to Andy, cursing at him.

I snorted softly and got to work fixing my decorations.

An hour later, my arms were sore from tying the wreaths to the points I'd identified before. Andy tried to keep himself occupied the entire time, but every now and then, when I glanced over at him, I'd find myself the subject of that sapphire gaze again.

Pretending his attention didn't affect me became my sole focus, which worked until I realised I needed to rehang three of the wreaths as I'd tied them off haphazardly.

"Okay, I'm done. I just have the ones for down the hall left."

I headed for the door, glad I was able to get it on my own, now my arms were unburdened.

"Wait– which room?"

I flicked open the order and read off a number, looking up at Andy's groan. "What is it?"

The grey outside deepened, the shops across the road already turning their lights on as I glanced at the window. Maybe he had a wife and kids that he needed to get home to? The idea sank heavy in my stomach as I stared thoughtlessly out of the window. Evening quickly sucked light from the day, and any remenant of residual heat along with it.

I wasn't looking forward to my walk back to my car. Frazzled at the thought of possibly seeing him again, I'd forgotten both my phone and my jacket on my last trip up.

At least I had managed to lock the thing.

"That office is up the corridor, through a locked door. I'll have to get a key from his desk..." Andy fumbled around at a desk across the room, yanking out drawers. Coming up empty, he turned to the wall behind, opening cabinets at random.

"I can come back tomorrow," I called.

Andy swung around.

"No, no, it's okay— got it!" He waggled a set of keys over his head in victory.

"Awesome." I grinned. I'd been delivering ornamentals all day, and I needed to get home to sort orders for tomorrow. My purpose-built refrigerator I'd sacrificed a study for in my house would hold them nicely until I could deliver everything the next day.

It was either that, or I had to get up very early, and morning was not my favorite time.

"Okay, let's get you sorted." Andy grabbed for the door before I could reach it, holding it open for me.

Andy and his good manners, always getting there first.

"Thanks," I murmured again, clutching my wreaths to hide my flush.

He led the way to a pair of metal mesh and glass doors that sat halfway along the corridor.

"The office you want is the next on the right after this," he said, reaching for the handle. "I'll have to lock up after you." He smiled apologetically, which quickly turned to a frown as the handle turned in his grip.

The frown deepening, he strode through the doors, checking offices on either side. Pictures of Texas Rangers ran the length of the corridor, both group portraits, and individual shots. The closest were in color but farther along the hall, past the rooms Andy was checking, they were sepia.

"Do you want me to stay out here?" I half-stepped through the doors, unsure.

"No. The office you want is that one," He pointed at a room he'd already checked. "Go ahead, Ella. If you need me at all, sing out." He pulled his phone out of his pocket, his long stride taking him down the hall in moments.

Feeling somewhat like a kid who was somewhere they shouldn't be, I stepped into the office Andy had indicated, making quick work of the remaining decorations. Satisfied with my efforts, I backed out of the office and straight into a warm body.

"Oh, Andy, I'm sorry—" My words died on my lips as my body reacted to the unfamiliar shape pressed against me.

My skin prickled as a quick glance over my shoulder confirmed my suspicions.

Dressed mostly in black, the strange man was tall and lanky, very different from Andy's well-formed bulk. His head tilted to the side as he assessed me.

"Should you be in here?" Amusement coated his voice, which should have sounded fine, but my skin remained prickling, every sense on high alert.

I gripped my remaining wreath.

"I was just, um—" I waved back into the room, then jiggled the wreath gently. "I think Andy's coming back to get me soon. If you needed him."

The man stayed still a moment longer, then smiled — a half-alive, slimy thing. "No, I don't need Andy." He watched me a moment longer, then turned and disappeared.

I blinked.

"Are you done here?" Andy popped his head in. "It's all clear up there. Are you okay?"

I shook my head. "There was someone, a man just here but—" Andy disappeared from the doorway. I stepped tentatively into the hall, disconcerted. Andy walked back from the double doors, shaking his head.

"I've got to lock up," he said with a strained smile. I nodded.

"Thanks for your help, Andy. Merry Christmas." I hesitated a moment longer, unsure what to say.

"Do you want to grab a meal sometime? Before Christmas, maybe."

"I have a lot of work going on right now, with the holiday and all. Which is only a few days away," I reminded him.

"It is?" Andy blinked comically.

I burst out laughing. "You were never good with dates." I grinned back.

"Nah, still terrible." His gaze fell on me again. "Let me take you out, Ella."

I swallowed back the words I wanted to say. "Maybe after Christmas?" I demurred.

Andy's face fell a little as he locked the doors, leading me back to the elevator. I glanced again at the Rangers lining the walls, picking out his father and grandfather this time. I raised a hand, almost touching the face that so resembled Andy's.

He pressed the call button before I could object. The doors opened with a ping.

"Merry Christmas, Ella. It was good to see you again." Andy gave me his trademark grin this time, and despite that his attention was clearly elsewhere, it still sent a thrill along my spine.

I stepped inside, wondering if I'd done the wrong thing, after all.

Andy nodded, waiting until the doors began to close before he turned and strode back into the office, the heels of his boots silent on the carpeted floor.

He was gone before I managed to open my mouth to reply to the most handsome Ranger there was.

"Merry Christmas, Andy," I whispered to the empty interior of the elevator.

CHAPTER THREE

ANDY

Focusing on work got harder the more I tried. Seeing Ella again after so long had thrown me for a loop. My mind whirred back to the day I had last seen her, when I was accepted into the Rangers. She had been so happy for me, so sweet with rosy cheeks and a smile I wanted to kiss until that enormous energy became something deeper.

There had been plenty of girls through high school, and a few in the last decade, but no one had held a candle to Ella. I'd spent years pining after her and throwing myself into my job...which had worked out just fine for my career. My love life, not so much.

"Head in the sandbox again?" A bag slapped down onto the desk beside me, apparently with the weight of half of Texas in it. But it was the accented voice that gave him away.

I raised my head with a grin. "Brodie! Merry Christmas, man. I wasn't sure you'd make it back in time."

29

"And miss Christmas at my Mamma's table? Are you fucking kidding me?" Brodie Martinez embraced me with one bare arm.

"I've heard it's legendary, that food. And put some clothes on. You're indecent."

"Been in the sun too long, you sayin'?" Brodie grinned through the tan he sported, though his skin had been fairly dark to start with.

Brodie Martinez was a Hispanic operative who dealt exclusively with the cartels. No one had seen or heard from him for months—except maybe for Archer, who wouldn't tell anyone, regardless—and we all assumed he'd be in Mexico over the holidays.

"Damn good to have you home. How long before you head south again?"

Brodie shrugged. "Couple of days, maybe. Long enough to make the family happy."

"Gotta give proof of life," Jake grinned at Brodie from his desk, though his smile was a little dimmer than it had been before.

Brodie nodded. "Short-lived, *güero*. Sisquo might be a stray dog, but a street mutt is smarter than a spoiled one. His accounts have lines that aren't the drugs. It

30

will take time. Maybe the year, unless I fluke a contact." He turned to me, and the message came across just fine.

If it wasn't just drugs, the millions of dollars worth we worked to prevent crossing into the US each year, then Brodie was likely looking as sex trade or human trafficking. Anything that helped build the case against Sisquo's cartel was worth the effort.

"You do what you need and get us the information as soon as you can. Don't compromise yourself, or the job."

Brodie nodded, his shoulders relaxing.

I was glad to come across as less of an asshole than he expected.

"Fuck, you sound like Ethan."

"Is that a bad thing?" Brodie's attention turned on the blond man.

Jake held his gaze for a second, then looked away. "If you want to be teacher's pet."

Brodie snorted, ignoring him.

I studied Jake. His jaw clenched, his fingers balled into fists. I was missing something with him, and I had the feeling that if I didn't work out what it was soon, the young Ranger would self destruct.

Jake had serious potential to be an incredible Ranger, if he put his mind to it. He'd made it into the most exclusive unit mainly on bravado and a string of solid cases, but he'd need more than that if he wanted to promote to head his own unit.

Brodie, on the other hand, was an exceptional operator, most reliable on solo missions, but I'd seen him work well in a team environment, too. Jake could do worse than to use him as a role model. I threw a note in Ethan's calendar to put him undercover with Brodie as soon as the holidays settled.

"Earth to Matthews. Andy. Where you at?" Brodie grinned at me, though his gaze sharpened as he studied my face.

"Nowhere." I ignored the heat that rose in my face. With short blonde hair, I looked resembled a tomato when I was embarrassed. "Henderson's been his usual assholic self."

"Liar," Jake cheerfully dropped me in it. "He's in lurrrve."

Tomato time.

I threw the last remaining badge at him.

Jake caught it. "That was a terrible toss, man."

32

"I'll show you what to toss," I grumbled.

"Good to be back." Brodie swept his bag from his desk. It clunked on the floor.

"What the hell is in that?" I eyed it. Knowing Martinez, it was likely something explosive.

"Space rock for my nephew. He's an enthusiastic geologist for a nine year-old."

"You brought a meteorite across the border? Did you declare it?"

"When was the last thing I declared what I brought home?" Brodie grinned, but there was a challenge in his gaze.

Fuck me if it isn't the season for testing limits.

"Would you be owning up to it if Ethan was here?" I snapped, running a hand over my head. Brodie's expression didn't change, but then, he didn't have to. "Sorry. Stretched a little. But try to uphold laws, not break as many as you can in a week."

"Thinking with your dick does that to you," Jake added in helpfully.

Brodie's grin widened.

"You two are fucking impossible." I groaned.

But every time Jake mentioned Ella, she sprang back to the forefront of my mind.

If I were honest with myself, she was there without his prompting. I had a feeling a sleepless night was in my future, with my hand as company.

Lights lit up the streetscape below, showing off the garlands that decorated the shops outside the warmth of our office. Neon Santas glowed lewdly in windows, and an inflatable sleigh was tethered to the roof of the coffee shop across the road.

An idea started to brew in my mind as I watched the twinkling lights, and the shoppers doing their quick step in a last-minute shopping effort through the crowd.

I powered down my laptop, eying the paperwork still in my inbox. I hadn't managed to get more than half my emails done. But this season had more in it than just work, if things went as I planned.

"Have a good evening gents." I grabbed my laptop bag. Emails could be done at home. I glanced at Brodie with a crooked smile. "Hope your nephew enjoys his space rock."

CHAPTER FOUR

ELLA

Roses that should have stood tall and perfect wilted in their vase, the tulips next to them in the same, sad condition. I groaned, running my hand over the cooling unit inside the large fridge my brother had installed inside my house a few years ago.

One of the fans wasn't working. I tapped the box, attempting to peer inside. Naturally, it was the larger one, which gave the unit its greatest cooling capacity. It gave a little groan, matching my own. Walking out of the fridge with my roses cuddled in one arm, I collected my phone to call Chad, hoping he could help.

When he didn't pick up, I sent my brother a short message, hoping the few words said everything I couldn't. I twisted one stem, wondering if I could use some of the unfurled flowers in another display, and hoped I had sufficient spares to make a new one, which brought back the memory of other crushed stems.

Recalling the image of myself on the floor, clutching my wreaths, I half snorted. Seeing Andy again had brought up so many memories and emotions I'd buried deep so long ago. I suspected that I might still love the sexy Ranger I had tried so hard to forget, but I refused to go there. I'd given him up, and I had no right to go barreling into whatever perfect life he had made after I had left.

That had been the whole point of breaking up with him in the first place.

The tiny bud rolled between my fingers and split. Scarlet petals flaked away as I rubbed my fingers clean. I put the flowers on the dining table with a small sigh and went to check the fridge for extra stems.

My workspace — in reality, my living space that I never used due to said work — was covered with a variety of dried and fresh displays. In lieu of an actual shop front, it was the next best thing besides my website to show potential clients what they could expect. Flowers had such a connection to the things people often loved most — other people.

They bought for special occasions: a loved one's birthday, wedding anniversaries, dates. Funerals. All times that built memories around those moments, and the arrangements helped to symbolise remember that.

Head down in my work, I didn't hear the bell the first time. The second — or maybe third — time that it rang, a deep voice accompanied it.

"It's unlocked," I called back. "Just come in. I'm out the back."

I tidied up the cut roses in their tall vase. They weren't exactly what the customer had ordered, but I was more than pleased with the long stems, and the flowers were ready to open in the next day or so. I swept cuttings into a wastebasket as heavy footfalls echoed down my cedarwood hall.

The house was reasonably new, and I'd been lucky to buy it before Cedar Park became popular. It was a safe suburb and though I'd love to spend more time in the mountains, having a steady business in a good neighborhood topped my desire to live on the land.

Besides, I could go to my parent's farm any time I wanted to see cows.

"Okay, there was a small mishap with the fridge, but your flowers are just fine, Mister, ah—" I shuffled printouts of orders with slightly damp hands. Invoices stuck to my palms, despite how many times I flapped. I let out a soft sigh, my focus waning.

"Matthews."

His deep voice stopped me. I lifted my head, staring straight into familiar, sapphire eyes.

"I– uh, I didn't think I had—" I floundered, trying to recall if an order had come through for that name. I would have taken note of anything potentially Andy-related, surely.

Pushing at my orders proved impossible with invoices still attached to my hands. Picking at them with my fingers only drew out my humiliation.

I groaned for the second time, the heat of a flush crawling its way up my neck.

"Let me help," Andy's voice filled with barely-contained laughter.

I tried glaring up at him, but with a cheeky grin like that, how could I even pretend to be grumpy?

In the end, the orders were back in their place on my desk.

"Thank you. Now, your order."

Andy cleared his throat. "I don't have one. Yet," he clarified, raising both hands in his defense.

I took a breath, waiting for him to explain, then changed my mind. "Wait one second." I grabbed my roses carefully, stowing them away from the broken fan in the fridge.

The temperature hadn't changed much, but it could be a problem if my brother didn't get back to me soon. Or I could call a refrigeration expert. That would be expensive, and though I made enough to pay for my house and expenses, I couldn't throw money at an emergency fix.

"This is huge." Andy peered into the unit, his arms hanging from the lintel above his head.

I jumped, my hand on top of the broken fan I was contemplating. "Yes. And it's not working well, so, shoo." I flapped at him again, but he took no notice.

"Not working well?" Andy ducked into the fridge, which really didn't have enough room for both of us to be inside it at the same time. Shelves lined the walls either side of us as we jammed in like sardines.

"What, you're an electrician now?" My temper ran short with him in my space. Flowers were my life, and if the entire unit blew up, I might actually sit down and cry. And moments like that required solitude when my dignity was likely to be on the floor.

"No, but I grew up around your Dad, and he might have taught me a thing or two..."

"Please, be careful," I begged, straining to see what he was doing, "it hasn't been a good morning. If this thing goes up in smoke, then..." I gestured around us to his back.

"Okay...let's try this."

My mouth dried. "What are you planning—"

A *whoomp* and a small bang came from where Andy hunched over the fan. He swore, jumping back, right into me.

I clutched for arrangements and vases that wobbled precariously on their racks. Andy grabbed for a toppling basket that shouldn't have been in the fridge to start with. I shook my head — it clearly wasn't screwed on tight enough today.

I'd been skittish ever since I'd bumped into Andy. That was a whole new rabbit hole on its own. I ranged from angry at myself to wishing I could return to the days before I left him. I straightened the vase last with my knee, glad not to have lost anything else today.

40

Including my temper.

I grabbed that slim tether tight, breathing hard through my nose. I looked up into Andy's grinning face, and the tether snapped.

"What are you smiling about? We could have broken everything." I waved my hands madly as he folded his arms, watching me with raised eyebrows. "And you shouldn't be playing with things you don't...understand." Andy moved aside, and my voice dropped to a whisper.

The fan swung around merrily, cool air blowing from it.

"You're welcome." Andy's grin was back.

I opened my mouth, closed it, and opened it again. Knowing I couldn't hold everything in without losing something important, I gestured wordlessly out of the fridge. Andy followed me, closing the door behind him.

"I'm so sorry," I blurted, turning back to face him, coming nose-to-chest with his shirt. I took a step back and bumped into the fridge door.

Andy followed me. He caught my chin, drawing me up to meet his gaze. His fingers brushed lightly over my jaw, sending

41

a million sparks racing through me. My lips parted, tingling as I leaned into his hand, my head dropping back a little. He dipped his head, and just as I thought — *hoped* — he would kiss me, he dropped something long and thin into my hands.

Andy stepped back, taking the warm air with him.

I managed to breathe, looking down where his hand cupped mine. A mangled stem — *I wasn't even sure what sort* — lay in my open palm.

"This little guy nearly cost you half a year's income. I didn't make a miracle, Ella, I just yanked that thing out. Sorry I backed into you, but I didn't want to lose my digits when the fan started up again."

He wiggled his fingers around mine in a familiar motion. Goosebumps rose along my wrist, the skin hypersensitive to his touch. Andy's fingers followed their path, tracing lines along my arm. I shivered as he drew me into him.

You can't do this, Ella. You left him for a reason.

But it was a terrible reason, and I never should have done it.

He doesn't have time for you.

42

Logical me lay down a list of reasons in justification, but when he was so close to me, they all fell apart. My mind was shoved aside by my heart. Andy's breath brushed my lips, goosebumps rising over me everywhere.

My table vibrated. My phone buzzed merrily in its overcrowded space. My hazy brain couldn't put that together — until I peeked around Andy and saw the number — my next order, the one I'd expected Andy to be when he walked into my house.

"Excuse me," I said hurriedly to Andy, slipping beneath his broad arms, wishing I could stop and touch him, to rediscover the man he'd become.

I picked up the call, Andy's sigh drawing a shiver down my spine, his fingers trailing along my arm. Trying to focus on what changes the customer needed, I took note after note. Finally, my customer finished talking and gave me a delivery address for an hour's time. He ended the call without checking if I was okay with it — I'd barely make it across Austin in that time, let alone make changes to his arrangements too.

And I needed some rose petals. I had those. I knew I had them. Somewhere.

Where?

Hunting around my living room, I lifted things, rearranging everything.

"Can I help?"

"Andy! I— I need to focus on work. I'm so sorry, and thanks so much for helping me, but I really do need to get this done. And I need to make changes, too..." I pulled out drawers I knew didn't hold rose petals, my search entirely fruitless.

Two strong hands closed gently around my shoulders, his body warmth wreaking havoc on me even with the thin barrier of our clothes between us. "Ella. Tell me what you're looking for."

"Rose petals," I gave in with poor grace, holding up my hands. "There should be these big, clear plastic sachets of dried rose petals. It's for an anniversary. I have to get this—"

"Go, do. I'll find your petals."

I dashed into the fridge, madly finding the flowers from my spares stack — I'd need another trip to the markets tomorrow morning, and made a mental list to order from a specialist grower — and made the changes. In record time, I popped out of the fridge, closing the door carefully behind me.

Andy leaned against the hall wall, dangling a stack of rose petal sachets from long fingers, his sleeves rolled back. Heavily muscled forearms stood out beneath his cuffs. He had always been fit but this was just...divine. I brought my attention back to the job at hand with effort.

"Oh, my god. Thank you. Where were they?" I headed for the car, grabbing for my keys and bag, but he got there first.

"Go," he directed me, following me down the hall. "They were beneath the order sheets. They got covered up when you flapped at me. I think."

"Oh." I couldn't think of anything else to say. "Well, thank you."

"Ella—"

I ignored him, bundling everything carefully into my small car parked next to his Chevrolet Silverado. His oversized truck made my little blue car covered with its white decals for my business look ridiculous.

A part of my brain looked at the two vehicles parked on the drive together, where they might have been every day for the last ten years if I hadn't decided our futures for us both.

"I'll um, I'll—" I ducked into my car, turning the engine on. Andy ducked into my driver's window. I shrieked, flapping at him.

"Would you please stop doing that!" I cried, batting him with every word for emphasis.

"I really did come to order flowers."

"Oh. Um, who for?"

Your girlfriend? Fiance?

My heart was going to be broken in this, I knew it, somewhere beneath the heartache that was all Andy.

Well, that's called karma, Ella. It's what happens when you break a man's heart for no good reason.

I'll give you a good reason.

Snarking at myself wouldn't achieve anything, except giving me a headache. But I *had* broken his heart. Maybe it was time for it all to come back around to me.

Not that there really had been anyone else since him. In ten years, I'd gone on a few dates, had been kissed once. I'd tried to enjoy it, but the cute man just looked like a boy as I compated every date to the benchmark that was Andy. It was never the same and it was never better. My love life was officially past its use-by date.

"Mom. She's still out on the land. She'd probably love to see you."

When there was no mention of a girlfriend, my heart leaped, then I

46

remembered the last time I'd seen Rachel, hugging me after his graduation.

"No, she wouldn't," I said sadly. "Will you send me your order please and when you'd like me to deliver it? I really do need to get across town."

"I don't have your number, Ella."

Remember?

His eyes said it all. My face flaming, I dug about in my handbag, extracting a business card. Still wearing his heartache on his face, with the muted entreaty for answers I knew he was too kind to demand, Andy waited with a grace I knew I would never possess.

I handed the slim card to him, letting it go too fast, relieved not to see bitterness or anger directed at me in his face.

"My number is on there. It's the only one I have."

"Mmhmm. You won't block me?" Those words could have been terrible, but instead, Andy paired them with that contagious smile, his eyes sparkling.

I let out a breath a moment before my lungs burst. "No. I promise."

He nodded, stepping back, placing his hat on. I backed out of the short drive, taking care not to run into his truck, and headed for the other side of Austin, my heart pounding.

He'd nearly kissed me in my own house. What in the hell was I doing?

And I'd just given him my phone number — which seemed like a lot more than just the flowers he was ordering for his mother. I shook my head that he'd come to me for that, or was it just an excuse? My heart leaped a little at the thought. I'd pushed him away at his office, and now at my house, when he had been my knight in rolled shirtsleeves — with those fine forearms. Would he ask me out again?

Did I want him to?

CHAPTER FIVE

ANDY

My desk was finally clear of the fake badges. The things gave me a headache, rattling about whenever I moved paperwork aside for yet another menial task that crossed my desk.

It wasn't that both my captains had left to chase their own demons for Christmas that bothered me. I arched my back, stretching my arms over my head to relieve cramps building along my spine. It was amazing how much tension accumulated from driving a desk.

No, what bothered me was the lack of structure in my day. My usual workload consisted of longer cases, and in-depth analysis that ran for months until I worked everything to a satisfying conclusion.

All I did at the moment was pour a watering can over spot fires that kept springing up like gophers the moment my back was turned.

This type of piecemeal work was doing my head in.

My fingers twitched on my desk, the command of the unit for the holiday period sitting poorly with me. I was a capable Ranger; my heart was still in my career. But I'd never quite fit the highly decorated shoes left to me. Enlisting had still been my choice, and I'd make the same choice again, should I have the opportunity to go back in time. Though this time, I'd show Ella that I needed her with me. My first few years without her in my life had been rough, more than I'd ever shared with everyone. Dad had taught me the value of an amicable mask, and the hours of training and rookie work had taken most of my energy.

The pattern that had become my lifestyle in my early years as a Ranger hadn't changed much. I ran my hands over my face, staring ruefully at my inbox, which appeared to be fatter than it had been the day before.

You are a Texas fucking Ranger. Get your head out of your ass.

My phone buzzed beside me.

Mom: The flowers are beautiful. xx

I sighed, knowing I needed to call her. I pushed more paperwork aside, my phone vibrating across the small space afforded it. I snorted. Paperless office, my ass.

Mom: Ella looks as lovely as always.

I grinned, raking a hand through my hair. Ella *did* look good, and I fully intended to use the number she'd given me to ask her out again — before Christmas. I checked my calendar and grimaced. As that was only a few days away — make that *one* day away — I really needed to pull my finger out. How had I lost three days? Ella was right; I really was shit with dates.

Shuffling the piles of paperwork on my desk, I knew the answer lay hidden somewhere in their depths.

Mom: She's not wearing a wedding ring.

I sighed again and turned my phone over. Maybe sending Ella to Mom hadn't been the smartest move. She'd likely harp on the subject until I did something, and as distracted as I currently was, that might actually be a good thing for once.

"Get your head out of dreamland." Jake placed a takeaway cup on my desk.

I eyed it, suspecting he'd returned the favor in presenting me with a cold coffee.

"You've been long enough." I took a sip; yup — dead cold. Jake grinned at me from over the edge of the lid. "Flirting with the barista?"

"Nah, he wasn't my type." Jake winked and sauntered away, his good humour indecent at this time of year, in my opinion.

I scrubbed my face with my hands and gave a groan. I was becoming a Grinch. Or channeling my boss in his absence, maybe. Though Archer's bad days had the tendency to be the apocalyptic sort.

"Okay." I sipped the cold coffee, decided I couldn't stomach it, then drained the thing anyway. "What have we got left from this shit-pile, and what's new that's coming in?"

Jake leaned on the desk to my side, his own coffee steaming in his hands.

I frowned; had the younger Ranger actually waited for a second coffee just to let mine get cold? Or maybe he had been flirting, as I'd suspected.

"Smile, Andy. It's Christmas." He gave that slightly crazed grin again, and I remembered his nasty break-up only a few weeks past.

"How are things with...Sandy?" I stretched to remember her name. Jake went through flings like wildfire, but he'd been with his last partner for longer than we'd all suspected. "Have you heard from her?"

"Nah, blocked her. Don't want more vitriol poured down my throat, thanks. No one deserves that at this time of year. Or any fucking time of year."

"Sure." I stopped, not knowing what else to say. I'd never told anyone what had happened with Ella, not even my family.

I'd just shrugged it all off when we broke up. I focused on my career, as there seemed little else to pour my hurt into at that point, and buried the dreams of giving my girl a diamond ring for her graduation day at the end of the year.

"You hear Bill Landy passed?" The corners of Jake's eyes crinkled in a sad grin.

"Damn. I might go out and check on Maise later. Does she have anyone to help her run Kinland Creek?"

"I heard she might be going into a nursing home. Had a bit of a breakdown after the funeral. She's a fair way out at the edge of the mountain, though, if she's alone. Gonna be a hard Christmas. 'Specially for those of us doing it alone." Jake stared over my head, his eyes unfocused. "Fucking freezing this year. Might even get snow."

"Yeah, well. There's always space here for you, man." I didn't push him not to harp on it. I'd try to see Mom in the evening unless there was an emergency, which was likely — but December twenty-fifth would probably see me sleeping on the office floor at my current rate of work.

If I slept at all. Jake kept talking, and I struggled for a moment to refocus.

"You ever had family like that? When one was gone, the other just wasn't the same? I'd love to have something that solid, one day."

I snorted, tasting the cold coffee. "You need to stop sleeping with everything that walks by if you want that. God, you're a morbid bastard. I thought you told me to smile?"

"Yeah, well." Jake fell silent for a moment. "Caseload-wise, there's a little traffic across the border. The cartels know we close down at this time of year, so I reckon we might see movement there, take advantage of it. Stolen cattle, human trafficking, that sort of thing. Drugs will ramp up there come New Year's. It's their biggest profit. DV is on the rise. Again, time of year, right?"

I winced; domestic violence switched on something dark inside me. "Damn." I considered a moment. "DV isn't us. Pass it back to the local station."

54

It sounded heartless, but jurisdiction was what it was.

Jake grimaced, playing with his shirt collar. "It came from the local station. One of the cops reported his own partner beating on his wife. There's been an incident reported, too. Assault of one of the female officers in the same station house."

Shit.

If a uniform was assaulting his family or another officer, then that did put it smack in our path.

"You're kidding me," I swore under my breath. "Well, there goes my idea of a nice, quiet Christmas. Maybe the badges weren't so bad."

"Yeah."

"Alright, is there a team left to deal with the DV over this period?"

Coward.

I cautioned myself against pushing for it, disgusted that I was so willing to palm it off. My hand curled into a tight knot, knuckles stretching white with the strain. I didn't want to snap and become the very evil I tried to prevent.

Besides, a Ranger was meant to be above all that.

55

"I can get someone to handle it."
Jake's grin sobered. "It's crazy out there.
Silly season, my ass. More like hold-my-
beer-and-watch-me-fu—"

"What a delightful sentiment."

Twice in one week. Really?

I didn't bother looking at the door.
Muscles across my back bunched, undoing
the stretching I had done earlier. I refused to
acknowledge the shudder that tickled the
length of my spine. Only one Ranger had
access to these offices with a voice that
annoying. Though he thankfully worked for
a different company of Rangers.

A heavy silence settled over the
office.

I sighed, dragging my gaze from the
piece of the desk I'd been studying.
Christian lounged on the doorway, far too
comfortable in a workplace that wasn't his.
"What do you want, Henderson?"

"Still looking for your Captain,
Andy."

"He's off for the season." I planted my
palms on the scatter of misdemeanors
overpopulating my desk. "What is it you
want?"

*And get the fuck out of my damned
office.*

I didn't say it aloud, and when I rose, still holding Henderson's slimy stare, I knew I didn't have to.

"Just looking for some paperwork. And returning these."

He tossed something shiny my way. I caught the jingling bundle by reflex, not looking at them. The heavy silence returned to the office while my mind churned. There was only one set of large keys for this office — the ones leading to the closed corridor I'd taken Ella along earlier in the week that accessed the evidence lockers.

Though why Martinez had ordered a bunch of flowers for down the hall, I still had no idea. Brodie had ducked in and left again for that legendary Christmas table his mother hosted. She lived in North Carolina, about as far from her ex-husband in Mexico as she possibly could with Brodie stuck in the middle. Christmas was just a screwed up time for so many families.

I jingled the keys in my hand, doing my best not to crush them.

You wanted something to do over Christmas.

"Did you borrow these?" I kept my tone light as I addressed Jake, though I was seething inside. Those keys were my

57

responsibility. To have them unknowingly missing could cost us the security of our recent cases, and my job.

"Just returning them from that nice little coffee shop across the road. The one with the pretty servers." Henderson had the audacity to wink. But not at me — at Jake.

"Thanks for being so dutiful," I drawled, my palms aching to be drawn into fists and forcibly eject the other Ranger from my office. "Doesn't F Company have other duties over Christmas?"

From the corner of my eye, Jake shook his head. I ignored him.

"We're on stand-down, of course. I just wanted to make sure you were *coping* without us."

"Doing just fine here."

It was a lie, and we both knew it. Henderson tapped his fingers on the brim of his hat, nodding. "Merry Christmas, then."

Neither Jake nor I responded as Henerson slid around the doorway and out of sight.

"Asshat," Jake muttered.

"Every. Fucking. Time," I muttered, still staring at the empty doorway.

Ella's wreath wreath swayed gently above it.

"Yeah. Remember when he tried to pick a fight with—"

"He would have been flattened. We should have let him." I squeezed the keys tight in my fist and looked at Jake. His face was already red; it brightened when I placed the keys in a jumble on my desk. "Why did you have these? And why take them out of the building?"

Jake stared at me, redder than ever. "I don't really have a good answer."

I closed my eyes. "Jake, I don't care if it's the worst damned reason on earth. You've gotta give me one," I stressed the last part, but from the looks of him, Jake already knew he was in trouble.

I thought again of the unlocked hall doors and promised myself I'd check the evidence room to make sure nothing had been obviously disturbed.

He perched against the desk, mute.

My eyes closed, I wondered how to get whatever he was hiding out of him. That he might be doing something illegal never came into it, more likely that he was just doing something frowned upon. But if the area had been compromised, then without his answer, I'd have to report him.

"Come on, man. Give me something. I don't want to write you up."

Jake's lips pressed in a tight line, color fading from his face as it returned to normal. He'd been a little nuts in the wake of his breakup, but this was the Ranger I'd worked with for six years — the stubborn mule who would work his ass to the bone to get a job done.

Whatever he was hiding, it was important to him. I just hoped it wouldn't cost him his career. Or mine.

I rubbed the back of my head, working the problem through. "Alright, one last chance. Tell me." When my offer was met with silence, I sighed. At this rate, I'd be blasting the desert clean. "Fine. Go write it up."

Jake's eyes widened, his mouth parting. "What? You—" He cut himself off quickly, but I'd gotten the reaction I wanted. He still cared — and that gave me everything I needed to know about the situation.

"You heard me. Write it up, put it on my desk. Give me a reason, or you're on leave until Archer gets back. After Christmas. Else I'll have to work with Henderson, and that's not gonna fly."

60

Jake cracked a small smile at that. He headed for his desk. I puffed my cheeks out. If I got him to handwrite it, I could destroy it. If it came through the emails, there'd be a trail, and I couldn't help him then.

"And Jake?"

He turned back, half looking over his shoulder.

"If you make shit up, you'd better make it look good."

CHAPTER SIX

ELLA

White daisies flared against the deepest red of my display, but the wreath was far from a celebratory one. Maise Landry had called to order the flowers herself when her husband, Bill, when he passed a few nights ago. Her voice shook through the entire call, and I'd had damp cheeks of my own by the time the entire time.

The funeral had been a small affair, as neither of the elderly couple had any surviving family. There were only the few ranch hands that had helped with their prime stock, and most of those had headed to their respective homes for the season.

I hadn't been able to stay, giving Maise a hug at the door as I left, sending up a few heartfelt prayers. Bill had always been around throughout my childhood, helping Dad with breeding and selling cattle when he first started out on the farm. For him not to be in the world any more cast a shadow over that corner of my life.

Maise had ordered plenty of decorations for the funeral parlor, but none for her own home, and I suspected the bill may have sent her broke. Kinland Creek cattle were some of the best and most valuable around. But they only managed a small herd of prime animals, destocking as they grew older together, and I doubted Bill had been doing much with them in the months before he passed.

I refused to take more than the cost in payment when I'd worked it out and wanted to give her something for her home, too. So I'd made up some extras to take out to her with large-printed instructions on how to preserve them.

I bounced messages with my brother, a small shiver going through me every time my phone buzzed. Part of me hated that I had to constantly check the screen, but it never showed the name m y heart wanted.

He's probably busy over Christmas.
He's probably never going to call.
Never, never, never.

I put him firmly out of my mind, which lasted until the next time my phone buzzed. I rechecked it, my head driving me mercilessly to disappointment as I replied to my Mom.

My best friends were both out of town for the week over Christmas; one with family on the East coast, the other, gone to Scotland for a holiday — about as far as she could get from family.

I twisted fine cuts of wire over the stems, tidying up tiny sprigs until I was satisfied with the shape. My OCD played havoc with me when I eyed it critically. One side that just didn't seem right.

Tweaking and twisting until it was perfect — to my eyes, at least — I carried the wreath carefully out to my car, sliding it into the trunk. My hatchback opened to a flat surface, perfect for my displays.

It would take me a good hour to get out to Kinland Creek, maybe more if some of the main roads were closed off for Christmas display. Last year the parades had started just after lunch, and though it wasn't yet noon, Christmas could be a crazy time of year, no matter where you lived.

My phone buzzed again as I started the car. I gripped the steering wheel tight, then plugged my phone in, accidentally checking who the message was from.

It wasn't Andy.

Sandra: Scotland is the bomb. There's no one here. Get on a plane.

Sandra: NOW. Come and see me.

I grinned, shooting a quick text back.

Me: Bored or lonely?

Sandra: Pick one.

Me: I'm wearing your gift. Love the plaid, and the scarf is perfect for this winter.

Sandra: Enjoy. It's from Edinburgh. It suits the weather here better.

A little facepalm emoji accompanied her last message.

I laughed, my pensive mood lifting with her characteristic whining. Sandra couldn't stand being on her own, but spending Christmas with her family had been deemed a worse fate, and so she'd taken option number three.

The drive to Kinland Creek was a pleasant one. Traffic was sparse, though the sky glowed a bright blue for a high winter's day. A local station featured an early Dierks Bentley album, one of the few not playing Christmas music. By the time I'd arrived, I'd sung my way through most of my post-Andy collection.

The painful ghosts of our breakup were replaced with happy memories of the year we'd spent together. Some part of me was relieved I could still think back to who we'd been then and smile. The miles ran fast beneath my tyres, the property coming up faster than I'd expected. Pulling up, I frowned at the open gate. I jumped out to close it, hoping none of Maise's precious cows had wandered out, and parked in the shade of the large barn adjacent to the house.

Behind the barn, the open forest land closed in quickly. A harsh, razorback ridgeline framed the land opposite the open pasture Kinland Creek was famous for. A tributary of the Colorado River coursed along a shared boundary line. It was just far enough out of town to be remote. Maise and Bill raised quality cattle, enough to be comfortable in their home together on some of the most beautiful land around.

The mountain range rose behind the house, offering a magnificent backdrop to the property. It would kill Maise to sell it, but if she needed money, she'd have a very healthy retirement fund.

Maise's little Toyota was parked next to Bill's classic Dodge 880, fully restored in lurid green, the obnoxiously bright hood as glossy as the day he'd bought it. That car had been resprayed in its original color and polished every month of its sheltered life with a single owner.

The same car he'd driven on their wedding day, I reflected sadly, remembering the photos that lined the farmhouse hall.

I collected the wreath from the trunk, a small doubt crossing my mind. Was I doing the right thing? If nothing else, I could offer to have tea with Maise. Maybe she wouldn't want company for too long, but if nothing else, I needed to check on her.

For over half my life, she and Bill had been family to me; it was my responsibility to make sure she was okay. I crossed the drive to the house, noting a few hands herding cattle into a small yard where two large trucks waited. Giving a wave and a smile in their general direction, I turned my attention to the house.

The house was closed up, which was unusual for Maise, who always had an open-door policy. Had she had a turn after Bill's funeral?

My skin prickled with alarm. I ran the last few steps up the covered porch without tripping, rapping the door until my knuckles ached.

"Maise?" I called, trying the handle on the screen, but even that was locked. A sense of foreboding rolled over me.

I should have come out earlier. I should have called.

"Maise! It's Ella," I yelled, hammering the screen. "You can let me in."

I stopped, my words sounding stupid in my own ears. The back door mightn't be secured, and I was worried she'd had a stroke or barricaded herself inside. Grief did funny things to a person.

Puffing out my cheeks, I balanced the wreath in my arms as I turned. One of the ends of the porch ended in a closed gate, but the other wound its way around to the back door. Was it to the left or to the right? In my panicked state, I couldn't remember.

I walked around one side of the square building only to end up at the gate. Muttering curses to myself, I turned back around, aiming at the other end of the porch. At the corner, I came face-to-face with an oversized cowboy dressed in bright blue denim, head to toe.

That look went out in the nineties.

There wasn't a skerrick of dirt on him, but somehow, he made denim a dirty word. The cowboy might be dressed like Justin Timberlake on his worst day, but JT had never looked so rough.

69

I cursed myself for my uncharitable thoughts. Pasting a smile over my shock, I gripped Maise's wreath too tight, crushing the little petals between my fingers.

"Wow, you startled me there. Bringing in the cows for Maise, are you? Destocking after Bill, huh..." I trailed off when the man stood expressionless and unmoving before me. "Um, speaking of her, have you seen Maise? I just came by to give her this." I waved the wreath energetically, daisies, and roses bouncing together.

The man stood silent.

I twisted the wreath in my hands, casting about for my next poor excuse at conversation

"She's gone out."

If I hadn't been staring straight at him, I wouldn't have believed this stone statue of a behemoth had spoken at all.

"Oh. Well, I'll just um, put this by the door then." A thought occurred to me. "Unless she left you a key?" I asked, hopefully.

"No." Still no movement.

"All right, then." I backed away discreetly.

Maybe not so discreetly.

70

I reached the front door, still backing up without taking my eyes off the clean and dirty cowboy, and laid the wreath on the stoop. Holding the fake smile to my face with aching cheeks, I waved in a somewhat friendly manner, jumping the last few steps.

The distance to my car looked like the extra lap on sports day, all open and breezy. Walking across the bare dirt was distinctly awkward. The hairs on the back of my neck rippled with sensation. Certain that the man was still watching my retreat, I refused to turn back to look at him, praying no one followed me.

I had my hand on the curved edge of the trunk to close it when my ears caught the noise. Growing up on a farm, a girl never forget the sound when her father cocks his rifle to put down her favorite, albeit ancient, cow.

That memory may have saved my life.

The shot reverberated between my ears instead of my brain as I tore around the corner of the barn, keen to put as much thick metal and other objects as I could between the stone man and me.

I stared around for inspiration, my heart pounding. Adrenaline flooded my system as I shifted into flight mode.

The tree line beckoned as a means of escape; only a few feet of open space between me and a sparse amount of cover. Without thinking it through, I sprinted away from my hiding place. Blood roared in my ears, dulling the shouts that broke the silence behind me.

An engine roared to life as I hit the tree line, dodging behind the tree trunks. Bark pierced the air around me, but I charged up the hill where I knew the forest thickened into heavy tree line. Anything that could obscure the shots aimed up at me was a benefit, and my limbs pumped all the harder for it.

What was beyond trees, I had no idea. I'd once chased a loose calf up this part of the hillside and remembered vividly where the creature had stumbled on a rock. I'd spent the night sitting with it, binding its leg. But I had never ventured farther.

That same rock grew nearer. I didn't hesitate, but powered forward, charging over it in a great leap. Holly shrubs tore at my hands and legs, but the scratches were of little consequence compared to the bullets heading my way.

A crash in the undergrowth behind me announced the man's pursuit. Maybe more than one? My breath was already screaming in my lungs for release that wouldn't come. Heat rushed over me in a flush that prickled my skin with a heady mix of fear and adrenaline.

I raced to the top of the incline, cresting it as a last shot rang out. My feet propelled me forward in a long dormant survival instinct, and the hillside disappeared beneath my feet in a sudden drop-off.

Conscious thought abandoned me as I tumbled into nothingness.

CHAPTER SEVEN

ANDY

Lines blurred before my eyes. I shook my head, but I couldn't focus on the screen no matter what I did. Yawning, I looked down at my watch. Midafternoon on Christmas Eve and even the coffee shop was ready to close up soon.

There was no way I'd be finished up by then. My inbox still overflowed, and I kept checking my phone for Ethan's call. There were a half-dozen small jobs to tick off my constantly growing list I couldn't ignore.

Besides, with Jake refusing to give me a reason for his behavior, I didn't have anyone else to cover for me. He'd left just under half an hour ago, and already the work seemed heavier. I refused point-blank to call Henderson in, although it might make the time pass faster. A and B company had officers on for the night, but they were on the other side of town.

We were so short-staffed this year there literally wasn't anyone else to cover the shifts. And the others had homes to go to; family. I had family, just not the one I wanted. Had wanted.

Still did.

I'd never called Ella, though Mom had pestered me as predicted. I knew she'd ask me about my run in with my ex-girlfriend tomorrow, assuming I made it to Christmas lunch. Or dinner. Damn, she'd cuss me if I didn't turn up at all.

Career first.

Dad had pushed me for it; pushed me into becoming a Ranger. Having secured an early retirement for himself, he'd loved the job, and I did too — he just hadn't told me the cost of it. Or maybe he'd never experienced it himself, with a wife and kids at home, waiting for him to return each night, regardless how late he walked in the door.

Or if sometimes, he didn't.

By the time Dad had reached the peak of his career, I had Ella as a single-woman support crew as a welcome distraction from my studies. As I started my own career and lost her, Dad retired.

The Major had left formidable bootprints to fill, though not as big as his father's. Third generation Texas Ranger. It was something no one else in the service could currently boast — something no one else currently dealt with the daily pressure and expectations. Chief of Staff Vincent Michael Matthews was inducted into the Ranger's Hall of Fame in the nineteen-fifties. I'd been weaned on Grandad's heroism as bedtime tales.

Though I knew I was nowhere near the standard of Ranger my family had held, I worked with the best there was for my generation. And for that, I was grateful.

My phone buzzed over my desk, the battery symbol flashing frantically. My charger was hidden beneath a pile of files somewhere. I picked my phone up, still dwelling in the past, flipping it over in my hand.

Jake's number came up.

I answered the call with a frown. "Aren't you supposed to be at home by now?" I asked, biting the ends off my words.

I was still pissed at him for not giving me a story — concocted or otherwise — and for leaving me in the lurch at a potentially critical time of year. Plus, I valued my sleep.

My sanity, not so much.

"Shots fired at Kinland Creek. Two cattle trucks were seen leaving the property ten minutes ago, and a blue bubble car, white writing down the side, florist or some shit. No plates or IDs yet. I know it's not us, but the uniforms are tied up and seeing as it's Christmas Eve...I thought you'd want to know."

Jake didn't say anything else, but I knew what was in his mind — he'd seen me moping over Ella for the last week, had likely seen her car when he got my coffee the day she was here.

I swore, standing abruptly to search for my hat and keys. The cattle rustlers were probably long gone, but...that blue car, with the decals — what was the likelihood it was Ella? Bill and Masie had been like family to her. It wasn't much of a stretch to imagine her going out to the property.

"Shots fired? What about Maise — has anyone checked on her?"

"She's in a home, Andy. Apparently, she was put there yesterday; the funeral was too much of a stress on her."

"Okay. That's terrible, and I'm sad for her, but at least she's not home. So, what's—" I cut myself off. If Ella was out there, she was likely checking on Maise and had no idea she'd been moved.

"Yeah, I reckon that's why rustlers have moved in, as soon as the place was vacant."

I ground my teeth together; Jake was right. Kinland Creek cows were worth a fortune per head, and easy pickings if no one was there to watch the place.

"Fine. I'll head over—" The phone on my desk rang. "Just a minute, Jake. Yes?" I picked it up impatiently, knowing it would be the same information Jake had already given me.

"Ranger Matthews? There's been a disturbance in Barton Hills. A domestic violence call—"

"Yes, Jenny, I know about— Wait, what? We don't do DV." My mind fuzzed on the rest of the information she dealt out.

"There's been a domestic violence call at Barton Hills. It's the home of a local cop, and this is his second report. Do you want to take it, or do you want me to send Ranger Masters out? He's standing right here."

"I got it!" Jake yelled over the line. I realized he must be standing in the foyer where the calls came before they were redirected to our unit. Static assailed my ear.

"You take Kinland Creek. I'll call in when I'm done."

"Thanks, Jake."

I found my hat and hit the stairs running, not caring to wait for the elevator.

———◆◆◆———

I inched my way out of the city, leaving the CBD for the day with half the town and thousands of last-minute shoppers inundating the row of shops in the main street. By the time I hit the highway, I had pressed my foot down, something about the whole thing bothering me, though that could have been my relief that Jake was taking the DV call, and guilt over not handling it myself.

I shouldn't have let him, being on the report, but without calling in one of our juniors over Christmas, there was no one else. I was overstepping my own jurisdiction by a large mile, not passing the Kinland Creek call on to the nearest precinct. Still, if Ella was involved, I didn't trust the local cops to not get under my feet. Their process was a fixed one; I had more leniency.

It would be a quick check around the homestead, chat with the neighbor who had seen the trucks. But by now, there wasn't likely any cattle left to worry about. I called ahead to the state line — border control might get them if they were leaving the state today.

Part of me wished Brodie was still around, but he would be at his mamma's house by now, enjoying time with his family. I couldn't call him back for some cows, no matter how pricey they were. The rustlers were more likely a reasonably local farm and would try to rebrand the stock to sell it off as their own.

My phone beeped in my ear, disconnecting as it went to low power mode. I dug around for my charger, clutching the steering wheel, then remembered I'd taken it up to the office earlier. Which meant it was still in Austin.

I was on my own.

I pulled into the drive at Kinland Creek, finding the gate wide open. Grabbing my phone, I took a few snaps before the thing ran out of battery. The tracks were wide and blurred at the edge of the corner. It looked like they'd come out at speed. A little mound of earth was lumped to the edge

81

of the road where the trailer had swung wide as it exited the property.

My phone gave a half-assed vibration and died completely. I tossed it on the passenger seat in disgust.

The driveway was reasonably short, winding over a small hillock. The breathtaking view of the house with pastures stretching for miles was laid out before me, still green from the Colorado River flowing along one boundary regardless of the lack of rain. Thick forest land bordered the incline to the east, building into a mountain range I'd hiked dozens of times as a kid while Dad and Bill alternated talking cows and classic cars.

But what stole my breath wasn't the view.

It was Ella's car that was parked beside the shed with the trunk wide open, and no Ella in sight.

I pulled up hard, jumping out of my truck. The entire time I'd been expecting it, but hadn't really believed it would be her car here.

There were gunshots reported.

Jake's words echoed around my head as I scanned the area, but the property was uncharacteristically silent. A glance at the

house told me what Ella had been here for —
a bright wreath provided a burst of color at
the foot of the closed screen door. Maise, of
course, hadn't been at home. The cattle
thieves had moved in.

Then Ella had arrived.

She put the wreath down.

My mind shouted the same
information over in my head on repeat. I
looked around for the cattle truck, but there
were no other vehicles visible in the yard.
Ella had been at the house. She had put the
wreath at the door. Then what did she do?

I traced her imaginary path down the
short flight of steps from the porch, across
the open ground to her car. The rustlers had
seen her. Had she spoken to them?

I placed my hand on the trunk, trying
to work out what she'd witnessed. Where
she'd gone.

A flash caught my eye. I looked in the
window to the driver's seat where her phone
sat, vibrating madly. Apparently, I wasn't the
only person who needed to find her.
Sandra's name flashed up, but she would
have to wait. Ignoring the buzzing phone, I
returned to my assessment.

Nothing in front of me stood out as
unusual. I closed my eyes, trying to picture

the scenario, but came up blank. They'd seen her, or she'd seen them. Had she hidden? But where did the reported gunshot come in?

Think, think, think.

I opened my eyes, turning in a semi-circle without moving my feet. Behind me was the rear corner of the barn. Studying the ground gave me nothing at all; it was far too hard and compacted to register footprints from constantly moving vehicles.

I lifted my gaze to study the vehicles, and the barn. The corner had a small dent in it. I traced the curve with my fingers, not really watching what I was doing, staring into the undergrowth around the edge of the tree line.

I wanted to call out, but something — *that same gut feeling as before* — held me back. My fingers caught on a jagged corner of metal, and I whipped my hand back with a sharp cry. The tip bled a tiny pinprick of blood. I frowned at my finger, my brain catching up.

More carefully this time, I traced my fingers over the jagged metal. Not a hole, exactly, because the bullet had grazed the extremity of the corner line, blowing out a small section just enough to make it appear

84

irregular. Looking back to the house, I lined myself up with its trajectory, looking straight into the forest.

A path of broken asparagus fern and crushed bracken led up the incline where the undergrowth thinned in the tree line as it became rockier. In my mind's eye, I watched Ella race up the hill, followed by whoever had shot at her.

I unholstered my gun, cocking it as I approached the forest. A flash of red caught my eye. I spun, raising my gun to aim at a pair of motorbikes lying on their sides in the short grass beside the barn. I memorized the plates in the event they were gone by the time I found her.

If I could find her, and there were at least two of the bastards out there hunting her with an icy Christmas closing in. The afternoons were short, and nobody wanted to be caught on the ridgeline once evening fell.

I tore up the hill, working for a mix of stealth — at which I was sure I failed — and speed as I watched the ground for tracks, not wanting to go off course and miss her path. It was a big mountain to search. Fortunately, Ella's speed and desperate dash made her easy to track — that meant it was easy for the other men to track her too.

She's already been running for an hour. Or more.

Ella was fit, but gym-type fit. I was pretty certain she wasn't used to the adrenaline release that came with a flight reaction. I leaped over a pile of rocks, checking for blood as I ran, but there was nothing to see.

At least she hasn't been shot. Yet.

The trees around me showed bullet damage around my shoulder height, some lower. They'd taken a lot of potshots at her by the looks of it, which reduced the amount of ammo they had left, depending on what each man carried. Assuming there were only two of them.

I hoped.

I crested the hill, windmilling my arms at the edge of a steep drop cut out of a section of granite outcrop at the very top. Topsoil crumbled away beneath my feet, dropping the few feet to the rock strata below. I edged along to a place where I could drop down safely. Looking back up, it might have been a two-story drop, and I was glad I hadn't made the jump.

My foot caught a broken stick as I searched the ground for tracks. Crouching, I nudged the long splinter. Its jagged tip was stained bright red, maybe an inch along its spiked edge. Half a sapling was bent in half beside it. Had she fallen onto the thing? I suppressed a snort. Yup, that was my Ella.

My smile soured, thinking it through. Breath hissed between my teeth. I hoped it was one of the men pursuing her that had fallen on it, but in her distress, it was more likely Ella. She was running on adrenaline, injured, and unable to stop. My hands trembled with a combination of fear and rage. In my mind's eye, I watched Ella run over the crest, miss her footing and tumble down onto the rock below, trying not to hear the crunch of bones that would come with such a propelled drop.

Or maybe she'd skirted the drop, knowing it was here all along, and one of the pricks after her had fallen instead. The ground here was covered in pine needles, with little undergrowth, but it made tracking their path so much easier.

Two sets of tracks led away from the drop-off, heading in different directions. I chose the one I hoped fit Ella's smaller-heeled boot print best and headed off after it, hoping I found her first.

The thought of finding those who hunted her lit something dark inside me, and I was glad Jake had taken the DV callout instead of me for more than one reason.

CHAPTER EIGHT

ELLA

I pressed my back against a tree, wishing my head would thump a little quieter as I tried to listen for anyone chasing me. My hand pressed to my side, I took short breaths, the sound wheezing far too loudly from my mouth. I covered that with my other hand but ended up snorting instead. My eyes watered over my fingers, but I refused to give up.

Go with grace, Ella.

I snorted again, salt coating my cheeks as I started to giggle, but that hurt, too. It would serve me right if I got myself caught in a fit of hysterics. I berated myself until the snorts stopped, finally subsiding to intermittent hiccups.

I tried to move my hand from my waist, but it was crusted to my side just enough to make me wince. Too scared to look at the wound and too exhausted to overly care, I peered around my tree, wondering if I should make a dash back to

Kinland homestead, to the facade of safety that my bubble car offered.

But I'd trotted along for what felt like hours, even though it was probably minutes, hand pressed to my side until it ached too much to run. Slowing to a walk, I'd reached the large tree, its trunk a sort of cover in the open alpine forest, and with no one obviously pursuing me, I stopped.

The warmth of the forest floor soaked into the cool of the air that preceded dusk, and with it, nightfall. The thought of spending a frigid night alone in midwinter was less than attractive; while the darkness might hide me from the cattle rustlers, I would likely die of exposure, though with an open wound, I'd be a magnet for an animal hungry for a Christmas dinner.

Cursing myself for the hundredth time for leaving my phone in my car, I took a tentative step away from the tree, jerking at a snap as I stepped on a stick.

Probably related to the one who stabbed me.

My inner snark jumped out of me, jabbing at my tender nerves.

You'd be highly strung too if you'd just been stabbed by a tree.

I'd jumped onto the tree when I fell off the short cliff, running for my life.

Fine, I fell onto the tree.

The thing had been growing out of the rock, and I'd landed right on it, tumbling the twelve-foot drop the crest ended in as the men chased me up it. I had managed to roll numbly to the side, into a sort of ditch, and they'd miraculously missed me as I curled into a ball on myself, hiding in the shadow, attached to half a tree.

Once they had disappeared into the next row of trees, I'd tried to turn back to the homestead. Instead, I was terrified back behind my rock by the rumble of engines and yells from the rest of the rustlers. Fear had taken me, and I'd run again.

The ridgeline looked pretty good after that. I'd made my way steadily in the opposite direction the men had disappeared into, with the plan of turning around — eventually. But my feet had just kept moving, and with no phone and no watch, I had little gauge of time passing, apart from my aching legs and burning lungs.

The canopy above, a tight-meshed collision of intertwined branches, allowed only a few slants of meager late afternoon sunlight. My stomach rumbled, but that could be due as much to the exercise of hauling my backside up the mountainside as it might be to time passing.

I made it to another tree, leaning against its side, and hoped the men wouldn't circle their way around the paths and come up ahead of me. With the cliff face on my left, there would be little chance of escape.

Their shots chasing me up the incline away from the Kinland Creek homestead still rang in my head. I blocked out most of the forest sounds, my head reverberating with the echoes of bullets ricocheting off trees around me.

Except for the crunch of footsteps somewhere to my back.

My shoulders jerked. I took a long, slow breath, trying to work out which side of the tree the person would come around. Were the footfalls heavy, denoting a larger person? Maybe it was a wild cat. Or a wolf? That would almost be a preferable option.

I shook my head, my muddled mind disorientating me.

Too scared to peer around the tree, I wound my fingers around a thin stick not too far removed from the one I'd impaled myself on, my side protesting as I slid down the trunk in a controlled drop.

Jagged edges bit into my palm, reminding me of the thorn that had pricked my skin the day Andy had come to see me.

Andy.

I wanted to see him again. Suddenly all my reasons seemed so stupid, so...inane. The man had a career — if he was with me now, would it matter to him what business I ran, what side of town I lived on?

Of course, it does.

I pushed the little voice away, determined to make it back to the ranch house, and find Andy. If he still wanted me.

The footfalls crushed leaf mulch nearby. Louder, this time. I straightened with a concerted effort, positioning my thin stick as my poor form of defense. My heart beat a staccato rhythm in my chest, surely audible to anyone around me.

With my side protesting, I came to my full height.

The footsteps paused beside my tree.

I listened, but I couldn't even hear a person breathing. Had I imagined the entire thing? Not stopping to second guess myself or to draw breath, I swung around the trunk with a war cry that could have brought half the mountain crashing down on me.

A flock of birds startled from their perch in the naked tree above me as I focused on my assailant, jabbing with my pathetic defense.

Brilliant blue eyes flared, broad hands raised to ward off my attack, though I only stood to his shoulder.

"Whoa, girl. You don't need that." His smooth voice rippled across the forest floor, carpeted with its heavy burden of matted leaves.

My chest heaving, I lowered the stick, surprise then exhaustion replacing my fear in short order. Pain ripped through my side. My fingers uncurled from their death grip, allowing the stick to fall to the forest floor.

I pressed my hand back to its place over the wound, staring at him as that same hand began to tremble. "Andy. I– I thought—"

"You thought I was one of them."

I nodded, adrenaline leaving me in a rush, taking my short burst of energy with it. "Yes." Exhausted more than I could ever remember being, I leaned against the tree trunk, its rough bark digging into my skin. A breeze ruffled my hair. I knew it should have an icy edge, though I barely felt it.

94

"I've been running around this ridgeline looking for you. You're damned lucky I chose the right set of tracks to follow." Andy kicked at a small clump of leaf mulch, his hands clenched into white-knuckled fists at his sides.

I eyed him warily, unsure if he planned on an attack-hug or shaking me.

"You don't need to take it out on the ground," I joked in a whisper, but my heart wasn't in it. My words fell flat.

Andy stopped, swiveling to study me with that intense gaze that had always drawn me to him. Rarely angry, he was a sight when fired up, though exasperated was the worst emotion I'd ever experienced from him.

Because you were a coward and ran away.

And he was a true gentleman and would never question my decision or pick a fight with me.

But that was a long time ago.

The words in my head were said in his voice. I blinked, wondering if he'd actually said them aloud. Did he still blame me? His mouth was moving, but I couldn't make out what he was saying.

95

I squinted, then leaned forward, trying to read his lips. It was a skill that still escaped me apparently, no matter how hard I worked at it. I huffed a breath out, leaning back. A small wisp wound its way between us to obscure his face, giving me a moment's reprieve. The forest darkened as dusk blanketed the remenants of afternoon light, taking the warmth of the day with it.

Andy leaned forward into my space, bracing an arm either side of me. My gaze drew along the line of his arms to where his jacket swung open to show defined muscle, even beneath his shirt.

Surrounded by the mix of soap and leather scent of him, I leaned further back, lost in his bright blue eyes. Memories of his arms around me that I'd stashed away arose, lashing their way across my mind until I couldn't define what was then and what was now.

How his body felt, pressed against mine, his eyes darkening into the colour of midnight when he showed me what desire and want really was.

This is not the time or place, Ella.

Regardless of what my mind screamed at me, I couldn't get away from the closeness of him. I didn't want to.

96

The warmth of his arms wrapped around me, bearing me to the ground for rest that I'd craved but hadn't allowed myself. Letting my head fall back into the pile of leaves was the highest luxury.

I inhaled slowly, sleepily, as his hands ran over my body, tugging at my shirt. Still wrapped in the scent of him, I acquainted my hands over well-muscled forearms I'd forbidden myself from remembering. I traced the lines of his hands, harder, more muscled than I remembered. Tendons stretched across their backs, his skin maybe a little rougher than the last time I had touched him.

My eyes drifted closed as his breath brushed the skin of my stomach, his hands pressing down. Gently, then harder.

Pain spiked along my side, over my chest. My eyelids ripped open, and I jerked upright, rising by reflex. I clawed at his wrist as I gasped for breath and found none, my throat closing up.

Dimly, I watched his mouth move, his lips tracing my name. The pressure increased, driving another spike of pain. White flared across my vision. The forest returned with darkened edges, his voice with it.

CHAPTER NINE

ANDY

"Oh, my god, Ella. Those bastards shot you." I pressed my hand over the blood on her shirt, hoping it was the right place.

"They didn't shoot me. I think. It was a tree," Ella gasped, color draining from her face though I wouldn't have thought that was possible.

She whitened further when I pressed down on her wound.

"Sounds about right." I covered my rising panic that warred for attention over a dark rage with a quick smile.

"Go easy," she rasped, her hand pressing over mine.

"Not a chance," I grinned back, surprising myself when I leaned down to kiss her forehead.

Her eyes widened, tracking my movement. Ella's chin tilted back, though she gasped slightly at the movement.

I hesitated for a second then drew back, fussing with her shirt. Tassels from her plaid scarf tangled around miniscule buttons.

I batted the threads away, but they swung back. Grabbing the annoying length of material, I would have pulled it tight, had it not likely strangled her at the same time.

I squeezed it in my hand, then unwound it from her neck, careful not to jar her, all the while cursing myself. Pulling a handkerchief from my pocket, I began to lift the hem of her shirt.

"Wait, what are you doing?" Ella coughed, pressing her hand over mine with a groan. "Ow."

"I'm going to use this," I held up her scarf, "as a bandage."

Ella straightened to peer down at my hand. "Is that– is it..?"

"Yes," I answered shortly, fingering the embroidered *A* on one corner of the folded square. I lifted the hem of her shirt a few inches to expose smooth skin on one side. The other was a mess.

Red smeared everything. I removed my hand, ready to pounce with the folded cloth as a dressing; I was relieved when the wound appeared not only to be just weeping blood, but also not too deep.

Grazes often made a mess, and were more painful than others. If the wound was deep, and there was little pain, then I really needed to worry.

I pressed the monogrammed handkerchief she'd given to me the last Christmas we were together — there had been an entire set of them at one stage, but now I had just one left.

"Stop staring, Andy. You're freaking me out."

"It's not too bad," I lied, flicking a few splinters and what looked like half a small tree away. She closed her mouth, breathing through her nose. I didn't have the heart to tell her this was the least of the pain she'd likely experience over the next few hours. "That's a hell of a branch you've taken on, Ella. But it's shallow, and it's clean. You're fine, baby."

The name I'd used with her in years well past slipped over my lips before I could think. She caught my eye as I finished up. To her credit, she didn't move an inch, her sharp inhales the only tell of her suffering.

"That's a good thing."

"Okay, I'm gonna tie this around you." I battled with the length of plaid, folding it double, lengthways. "Then we're going to head along the ridgeline for a bit. Okay?"

I wound the material around her toned torso, curved in all the right places, leaving enough to tie it tight just to the side of her wound. My hand brushed over her hip, hesitating. I tried not to look. It seemed an indecent thing to do with an injured woman, albeit one I knew well.

It's in the past, Andy. She left you, remember?

Her soft voice brought me back.

"We're not going back to Kinland Creek?" Ella asked in a quiet voice.

I looked at her sharply, my hands stilling over her skin, warm for now, but cooling quickly as the chill breeze I'd been expecting prickled over the back of my neck.

"Not tonight. It took me nearly two hours to find you. I can't believe you got this far in your condition." I pulled her thin shirt back down, covering the makeshift bandage.

"I might play with pretty flowers, Andy, but I'm not one of them. Wait. How did you find me?"

"A report came through to us of shots fired out here and a description of your car. There was no way I wasn't coming out to look for you."

I shot her a quick, sideways glance.

Ella stared at me from beneath her lashes, her bottom lip caught between her teeth. "Thank you. I– I didn't know Maise wasn't there. I should have called ahead."

"You couldn't have known." I filled her in on Jake's information, but left out his comment.

"Dying of a broken heart," she murmured.

"What?" I startled, surprised she'd followed the same conclusion as Jake had, too.

"You know. When two people live together so long that they can't live without each other," she finished, oblivious to my shock.

"I wouldn't know," I answered shortly and fell silent, not wanting to drag her into the blame that wrapped itself around my heart.

I could have had ten beautiful years with you by now.

A family. Children and a house. Not the townhouse I barely lived in.

I didn't blame her really at all; that fault sat solidly with me. I could have pushed her, approached her family when she'd ghosted me, but I'd taken her message at face value, forcing myself to believe the lie.

103

For Ella.

I wished I hadn't. It wasn't the me she'd known — what if she'd expected me to go after her? But the same part of my brain protested that *she'd* never reached out either, that *she* was the one who'd broken it off. I hated the way the blame sounded in my head. The same old doubts gripped my chest, drawing tight. A lot had changed in the last few years, but not how I'd felt about her. Never that.

She wrapped her hand around my forearm, holding tight as she eased herself up. I supported her lower back lightly. The girl with fire and clouds in her eyes had become a quietly fierce woman.

A hellishly sexy and beautiful woman.

I was falling for her again and didn't want to stop. Was it falling when you were already there? This time the hole seemed deeper, and I was on a trajectory straight to the bottom.

I just hoped it wasn't an oubliette.

Would she do the same thing as she had the last time we were together? Though I still didn't understand her motives, and that hurt more than anything else.

I led the way along the ridge, keeping just inside the tree line for cover. Leaf mulch crunched softly beneath our feet. A few stray ones drifted beneath the canopy, showering us in a light rain of the last reds the winter had to offer, bright against the contrast of evergreens that populated the mountainside.

Her back ramrod straight, Ella walked with a smooth stride for someone who'd landed on half a tree. I admired her tenacity, but while my heart was occupied with that thought, my mind let rip.

"Why did you really break up with me, Ella?"

The words tumbled out, though I tried to bite them back the moment I spoke. Her head tilted to the side, eyes bright in the last of the filtered sunlight flickering overhead beneath the swaying pines as the sun set behind the ridge.

"You were so perfect. Are perfect," she corrected herself, flapping one arm at me, the other pressed over the makeshift bandage wrapped around her middle. "But you needed your career. And you *didn't* need someone trailing along after you without a degree and with no ambition and," she gestured helplessly at her own fine frame, "well, me. Or someone like me," she added with a small frown.

105

"You broke up with me because of my *CAREER?*" I barked.

She shushed me quickly, swiveling on her heel to look around us, her fine features stretched in pain. "Yes. Well, maybe," she whispered, lowering her lashes to study her boots.

The same boots that were identical to the pair she had always worn. I wondered how many pairs of the things she actually owned, imagining a stack of boxes of fresh, calfskin boots ready for her to slip those gorgeous, long legs into. I fought back the shiver that crept over me, struggling to hold back my arousal at the image.

You have a job to do.

A job that had nothing to do with me fantasizing about my ex-girlfriend's slim legs sliding into brand new boots.

I shook my head, but the image refused to dispel before my eyes.

"It was a shitty way to break up with me, Ella," I groused, forcing my mind back to my words.

Even grumpy was better than hoping for something she clearly didn't want. And what sort of reasoning was that? Political stature wouldn't even be considered for me in my job until I was at the rank I was now —

and it had more to do with my performance, than my social standing.

I had never wanted a perfect wife who hosted campaign parties and played golf at the country club. However, I knew family did come into it as a Ranger rose through the ranks. I studied Ella with new eyes. Had she seen that potential in me, even back then, when I could barely see my way past selection and basic training? One hell of a special woman.

She always had been.

Something stirred in the forest, and I quietened. Pulling her off the ridgeline, I crouched low in the undergrowth, pulling her with me into a small copse of saplings and a single, large shrub. I hoped it would be sufficient concealment.

I peered out to the incline above us. A shadow moved there. My hand went back to my gun. I slowed my breaths in a conscious effort, waiting. The shadow flitted, moving away, and I couldn't tell if it was a large animal or a man. I wondered that they didn't have someone coming up the back of us, but didn't dare move.

"I was thinking of you," Ella hissed. I jumped and made a shushing gesture. She turned a shade of puce I wouldn't have thought possible, puffing like a little blueberry about to pop.

I bit back a grin as she glared at me.

Inappropriate much, Andy?

She opened her mouth to argue, but I forestalled her, brushing my fingers over her cheek. Her eyes flared wide at the contact. She looked so cute. I buried the urge to pull her into me and kiss her soundly. "Shhh. I think there's more."

"Ohh," she sighed softly into my hand, settling into the touch.

Her breath gusted across my fingertips, setting the nerves there on fire. I left my hand on her for a moment longer, then withdrew it before I did something stupid.

Like wrap that silky hair around my hand and kiss her. My own mouth tingled with the need to feel her lips beneath mine, to hear the tiny noises I knew she'd make.

Concentrate, Andy.

The ground crunched again. I sought the source of the sounds as best I could while motionless, knowing the movement would give us away. The footsteps faded after a moment, heading off in the opposite direction. Ella's hand gripped my sleeve tightly through my jacket, her breath hitching. I suppressed the urge to wrap my arms around her, for now.

An icy wind with a warm tail gusted against my face, raising the hair on my arms beneath my jacket for more than one reason.

Though the clouds were still light and fluffy, just visible through the canopy, they sold the lie of the sunny, winter's day. But by this evening, the weather would close in, and I didn't want us caught out in it when it did.

I waited a few minutes longer, then wrapped my hand around Ella's smaller, finer one.

"Come on. There's an old Ranger station a little way up the range. We can hang out there until these guys give up."

Or until the weather closes in and we're stuck for God knows how long.

I dearly wished I'd taken the time to use Ella's phone to call the situation back to Jenny. Hell, I'd even accept Henderson's help right now. Preferably in the form of a medic and a helicopter.

If I was lucky, maybe Bill had put a radio in the Ranger station. It was an older one, not considered in use, and I knew we couldn't count on that.

Gravel and twigs snapped underfoot, far too loud for my liking. I kept one hand on my gun, the other firmly around Ella's. Her fingers squeezed mine. I looked back into those hazel eyes, eyes that trusted me to make the right choices for both of us right now. Eyes I could fall into and never climb back out from.

But first, I had to know.

"Why did you do it?" I drew her alongside me, not letting go of her hand, even when she tugged gently. "I know it was a lie."

Please tell me it was a lie. Because I've never stopped loving you.

"I told you why." She discreetly tried to pull her fingers from my grip but gave up when I glared at her.

"Explain it," I ordered because anything else would have been begging.

I wasn't too far from going there.

"I was trying to get you to focus on your career because it was so important to you." She stared at our joined hands.

I wanted to see her eyes, though I didn't need to see them for my heart to know she was telling the truth.

"Sending me an '*I don't have feelings for you anymore*' message then blocking me across *everything* ripped my fucking heart out." My blood boiled at the memory:

110

opening the message, reading the words with disbelieving eyes. Not being able to reply or call when I'd expected to take her out that night. Having already– I stopped that thought right there. "That was close to Christmas, too. Sorry. I shouldn't have sworn."

"It's okay, Andy. I– I expect you to be furious with me," she said it so softly, the wind nearly stole her words before I heard them. I tightened my grip on her, refusing to let her go again. "You'd just been accepted into the Rangers after graduation, and I was still in school. It's not like I'm smart, Andy. I wouldn't have done your career any favors. And it obviously flourished. Your career, that is. You– you got your dream."

She finally looked at me, her luminous eyes wide. Had she ever told anyone why she'd done it? I frowned.

My dream was to wake up next to you every morning for the rest of my life.

"Do you really think you're not clever, Ella?"

She nodded, a half-deprecating smile twisting her lips a little.

God help me, she was still as beautiful as the day I'd met her. More, maybe. I brushed my thumb over the back of her hand, appreciating the shiver that coursed through her.

Damned right, it was a lie.

The girl still loved me. My heart soared, holding the painful memories at bay.

"I play with flowers, Andy. Pretty things. I'm no rocket scientist."

"You run a successful business out of your home," I countered. That too plenty pof smarts. I'd seen too many small businesses fail before they turned over their first year, and Ella's had been thriving for years. I'd checked.

"I don't have a shop. I can't afford it." She shrugged the admission away.

"Are you kidding me? That back room of yours is perfect. People buy flowers for someone with some sort of emotional connection. Birthdays, anniversaries. Funerals. Those same people might walk through your house to order and see your displays. You let them see who you are. That connection is far more powerful than any main street, overpopulated shopfront."

I closed my mouth before I ranted further. Hell, this woman brought out something new in me every time I was near her. What had I been missing without her beside me all these years?

Ella said nothing, keeping pace with me. No small thing for the injury she sported, never mind being half a foot shorter than me. Eyes thoughtful, she studied first the landscape, then me.

"You really do believe that, don't you?"

I turned to her, finding both her hands with mine, holding tight. "Ella, I—"

A sharp crack in the undergrowth brought us both to the ground. Pressing a hand to Ella's back to hold her down, I raised my head cautiously, waiting for the next gunshot as my mind caught up with the sound.

Movement off our path caught my eye. A white-tailed stag stood tall only a few trees in, an impressive set of antlers decorating his head. I stared in awe, slowly rising, drawing Ella up with me.

She pressed to my arm, open-mouthed, her warmth seeping through my jacket.

The beast gave us a cursory glance, a moment of stillness possessing it, then it pawed the ground and wandered off.

"It's– it's so majestic," her voice lowered to a hushed whisper.

"You got that right."

113

"How many points was that?"

"Too many to count." I grinned; the stag must have been a true alpha, never beaten.

A rare sight, indeed.

We watched until he disappeared into the trees. I noted my eyes adjusting to the dim light. Overhead, it became difficult to distinguish cloud from shadow in the hazy gray of dusk that filtered through the canopy.

"We need to get to shelter. The Ranger Station should only be a mile or so off."

"A mile or so?" Ella turned raised eyebrows my way. "Couldn't we have just gone back to my car?"

"Nah, those guys will hang around for as long as possible, waiting for you. You can ID them, which means their time cattle rustling in this state or along the border is pretty limited."

"Oh," Ella said in a small voice, her steps still keeping in stride with my longer ones, but with less bounce than before.

She wrapped her arms around herself, though the breeze had dropped. Cool air sank with early nightfall, a chill that grew so gradually, it was dangerously unnoticeable.

114

As the cloud lowered, we'd get a blanket of warmth before the snow arrived.

But none of it would matter an inch if I couldn't provide cover for her before that happened.

"Come on." I slipped my arm around her shoulders, expecting her to pull away. Instead, she leaned into me. I closed my eyes at the sense of her there, wanting to say something but also not wanting to break the moment.

Even though her feet must have been sore, she kept up with the pace I set. Shadow darkened the spaces between the trees, and though I knew we could probably turn safely back to Kinland Creek, it was several miles hike over downhill terrain. Ella might not cope so well with that in her condition, and I didn't want to unknowingly risk tearing anything inside her that was damaged. The icy air kissed my neck again, and I flicked my gaze skyward. The weather closing in bothered me, too.

I didn't expect it to be the blizzard conditions that had already been reported in the north this year along the US-Canadian border. Still, I refused to bring Ella back with a solid case of hypothermia when there was a relatively safe shelter nearby.

Almost full dark had fallen by the time we reached the cabin. Ella stopped talking some time earlier, and I had given her the time she seemed to need, lost in my own past, and visions of a future I should've fought harder for.

I walked beside her, unsure if she was exhausted from her experience and shock or if she was lost in memories.

The cabin appeared as a vague structure in the hazy light. I struggled to adjust with the shadow and twilight as it combined in an all-encompassing grey haze. Patting at the door, I felt around the frame, knowing there should be a combination key box on it somewhere. My hands hit metal at the base of the door. I stooped, fiddling with the lockbox.

Ella lowered herself slowly onto a porch swing.

"Looks like Masie and Bill might have made some improvements on the place," I nodded to the swing with a grin. Ella gave me a tired smile.

"Looks like it," she said, her voice a thin whisper.

The cabin's outlook was an almost sheer drop-off that usually gave a magnificent view of the opposite ridge and the next Ranger station across the valley. Both were unmanned, more of a historical value than of common use.

Hikers often used the supplies inside, so we'd taken to locking the things up over the years. Because the hut bordered on Kinland Creek land, we'd given the combination to Bill years ago on the provision he kept the cabin well stocked and maintained.

A brisk breeze swept up the bare rock face, the black clouds overhead clearly visible for the first time. I shivered and noted that Ella didn't.

Ignoring the threat from above for the moment, I pressed the combination on the key box again, angst growing in my gut when it didn't open. I rattled it and finally gave it a whack that hurt my hand more than anything.

"Damnit," I swore under my breath, shrugging my jacket off. I pressed it over Ella, but she waved me away.

"Keep it," she yawned, blinking furiously.

I bent to kiss her forehead, and she leaned into me. "Bill's changed the combination." I sighed. "I could press keys

117

all damned night and never get the right one."

And the storm was closing in. Even if it lasted only an hour or so, it would be a freezing — not to mention dangerous — hike back down the mountain in frigid conditions. Ella wasn't dressed for it.

I draped my jacket over her, and this time she didn't bother to argue. The cold bit through my cotton shirt straight away, and I cursed for not having thought to cover her earlier.

"Why don't you try their birthdays," Ella mumbled, sliding beneath the leather of my jacket.

I straightened, cracking my back with my hands on my hips. Ella's eyes were barely visible above my collar.

"How would I know their birthdays, Ella?"

I pressed the material down with one finger to expose her tired eyes ringed with a tinge of purple. My exasperation faded instantly, though the knowledge that she wasn't shivering and her wound needed to be seen to spurred me on.

I dropped my hand, walking to the side of the cabin. A small window was set high on one wall above what could be a bathroom or toilet. Perhaps if I broke that, I could wiggle through and...well, the door wouldn't open from the other side. I stamped my foot on the hard ground, scuffing at the dirt.

If I didn't get her inside, we'd be traveling back down the mountain under cover of darkness, but fully exposed to the weather. A noise caught my ear. I blinked, trying to focus on it, following the noise to where Ella huddled.

"Babe, say that again?"

Ella rattled off a string of numbers, my mind slow to catch up with the pair of six-digit dates before she subsided back into the confines of my jacket.

I studied her for a moment. "You spent a lot of time at Kinland Creek, huh?"

The top of her head bobbed inside my jacket and she mumbled a reply that sounded a lot like *"Maise."*

"I'm sorry about her. And Bill." I said softly, realization dawning far too late as to what the place meant to her. The people.

I turned the dates over in my mind a few times to memorize them and pressed the numbers into the lock with aching fingers, hoping I'd heard her right. The first one didn't work. Muttering curses under my breath, I tried the second number. My fingertips slipped off the cool metal buttons, a slight tremor shivering through them.

I stumbled over the number once and got it on the second try. Sending up a short prayer, I pressed the trigger to activate the release. The tiny door popped open, revealing two keys settled in the bottom of the small opening.

Whooping, I collected the keys. I looked over to Ella for a victory dance, but her eyes — the little I could see of them — were closed. My mood sobering, I slid the key into the door, getting the right one this time.

It opened with a puff of musty but warm air. Relief surged through me alongside a boost of energy as I searched for a way to make Ella more comfortable before the rustlers found her, or the storm closed us in for the night.

Or both.

CHAPTER TEN

ELLA

Something fuzzy pressed against my nose. I pushed it away, thinking of my brother's dog, but it bounced back. I wrinkled my nose, resisting the urge to sneeze, and muttered at it, rolling onto my side.

The material shifted, releasing a cloud of scent around me. Fluffiness tickled my nose again, and I half sneezed, managing to inhale a cloud of the leathery aroma. My brain vaguely recognized it through a haze of pain that shot through my side and chest, every nerve ending screaming for a single moment.

Andy.

The thought of him brought me back to the present. Despite the dull throb in my side, I raised myself on my elbows, peering around. My injury stretched with the movement. I flopped back with a cry, but my lungs protested at that, too.

A pillow propped under my neck dipped with my efforts as I sank beneath a pile of blankets, warm, but exhausted. My side ached. Still searching for Andy around the cabin decorated in cow paintings and pink chairs with darker pink coverlets, I traced my hand gingerly along my side.

Probing as gently as I could, I pressed around the edge of my wound, surprised to feel a gauze bandage over it.

"This place might not be a Ranger Hut any longer," Andy came into view, "but it sports a first-class triage station. And a decent stash of tequila. Thank God."

He knelt at my side, his sapphire eyes boring into mine as he studied me. Broad hands slid beneath the blanket and under me. Taking great care as though I were a delicate and valuable object, Andy maneuvered me into a sitting position. I tried scooting back, but the motion left me gasping.

"Thank you," I whispered, my throat dry. I coughed to clear it by reflex, my vision instantly blurring. Andy gripped my hands, holding on until the pain subsided. I wiped stray tears from the corners of my eyes. "You're amazing. As always."

He gave me a familiar crooked grin. "You're the one who dragged your injured backside up a mountain. I don't think I get to claim *amazing* today."

He offered me a drink in a neat tumbler. Ice rested at the bottom. I wrinkled my nose when he pressed it to my lips.

"Wait. Is that teq—"

"Water."

"Oh."

I let him hold the glass, unsure how steady my hands would be, or if I could even move them that high. Reaching up tentatively, I was relieved when I encountered no pain. Andy passed me the glass, his hands hovering beneath mine. For once, I appreciated the safety net.

"What's the damage?" I cleared my throat lightly, blinking as the tears returned.

"Sure you don't want a dash of tequila in that?"

"Not yet. Maybe later."

Andy nodded, pouring two fingers for himself. "You'll be okay, Ella. The wound isn't too deep. There were enough supplies in the cupboard to clean it well, and the place is a lot warmer and better equipped than I expected. Looks like Maise and Bill have been using it as their own private holiday home. Not that I'm objecting right now. This place would have been pretty spartan, otherwise."

"Me either." I wriggled a little, wincing. "Though the pink is, um, overbearing. Could you help me take some of these blankets off? I'm overheating."

Andy unwound me from the nest he'd created, with me buried in the center. "Hang on." His brows dipped together as he fought with the blankets, finally peeling the last of them away. I stretched out my legs, grateful for the air flowing around the little cabin.

"It is lovely, in a country sort of way." I tried to rectify my uncharitable thought of a moment ago, grateful we had a warm place out of the weather to stay.

"If you like an excess of pink." Andy rose, adjusting the heating. "You were so cold you weren't shivering when I brought you in." He spoke with his back to me, and his voice muffled, though I could still detect the pain laced through it. The fear.

Something clenched inside me; I wanted him to want me after everything I'd done, but I still felt I couldn't — *shouldn't* — do anything about it.

"Thank you for looking after me," I said helplessly. Would I repeat myself all night? I shifted, trying to work out how to get up.

Andy glanced over his shoulder to witness my struggle, and within moments he was back at my side.

"Nope. You're staying put, girl. I didn't do all that bandaging for you to go and mess it up."

I lifted the hem of my shirt, ripped and bloodstained, to find a neatly folded dressing over my skin. He'd cleaned around the area well, with no trace of the dried blood that had itched so badly before he'd found me.

"Th—"

Andy pressed two fingers over my lips.

I raised an eyebrow.

"Don't you dare thank me again. Or apologize. I did my job, and besides," his gaze softened, his fingers drifting along my cheek, resting at the base of my throat, "I don't give a damn about your reasons, Ella. I care about *you*."

My heart in my throat, I was sure he'd be able to read the panic building in me. "You shouldn't," I whispered, horrified as tears prickled beneath my lashes. I closed my eyes, unable to write them off as pain this time. "I'm not the right girl for you."

"Do you get to decide that?"

"Yes." I opened my eyes, letting him see my tears though my chest protested, my heart thumping too loudly. "I do."

Andy rocked back on his heels. His blue eyes pierced deep into my soul, and I knew he could see straight through my lie, and what little bravado I managed to cover it with. He nodded once. "Okay."

Rising, he held my gaze a moment longer, then turned away, heading into a different room.

Okay?

Andy Matthews never said okay or gave up. On anything. Certainly not when it was something he wanted. Or someone. I knew that look very well, and it wasn't his *I'm-backing-down* look.

I doubted he even had one.

A small tumbler made its way into my other hand. I took one look down and shook my head, laughing.

"I said maybe later, Andy. I don't remember you being this pushy." I grinned, but he just shook his head, closing my fingers around the glass. It warmed quickly beneath my hand.

126

"It's medicinal."

I raised an eyebrow. "You can do better than that."

"No, really." He grinned back, though it dropped quickly. "There are no painkillers here. It might be set up well as a first-aid station, but Maise and Bill must be iron horses when it comes to injuries. Were," he added softly, looking down at his hands. "Bill was– and Maise–" The words seemed stuck in his throat. He coughed, clearing it.

I watched him, my heart swelling. "You never changed. Still the same Andy."

My Andy.

He didn't speak, luminous eyes saying everything for him. His mouth pressed in a line, he leaned forward.

My breath caught.

You shouldn't. You can't have him. Let him go.

I ignored my brain, sitting up a little higher, though my side protested violently.

Andy stepped back, his gaze still holding mine captive. "There's some cut wood out back. I'll bring it inside before the snow starts. Before it gets wet." He backed away, hands pressed to his pockets.

I followed him with my eyes until he disappeared. A door opened somewhere behind me, letting in a cold blast as he stepped outside.

What are you doing, Ella?

I huffed at myself, taking a large drink of the tequila he'd poured me. My vision blurred again, but not from pain this time. Well, not that sort of pain. Stifling a cough I knew would cost me, I swallowed the bitter liquid in a gulp.

It fizzled the length of my throat, its sharp edge giving way to a pleasant numbness that soothed the ache in my side, but not the one in my heart. Its absence was conspicuous. I shifted a little easier, peering around for the bottle as I finished the glass.

Andy kicked the door closed and busied himself at the firebox, kneeling on a thick, dusky pink and obscenely fluffy shag pile rug. Dry wood crackled merrily, and he turned the heating off completely.

"Glad they thought to heat this place up like the Sahara," I muttered, straining forward.

"You might be glad of it when it's eight below outside in a few hours." Andy turned back to me. "Whoa, babe. Steady up. I don't remember you being a hardcore spirits girl."

His hand clasped mine as I managed to lean forward far enough to get my fingers on the bottle cap. Andy perched on the end of the short couch, sliding beneath my legs slowly so as not to disturb my side.

I accepted the glass with a nod. "You remembered right," I huffed, settling back, the ghost of his touch tingling the back of my hand. Those same hands closed around my ankles in a gentle caress, tugging them over his legs as he settled beneath my feet.

I shivered, goosebumps covering my skin where he touched me.

Totally unsexy. Nice work on the seduction front.

"Maybe you haven't changed too much either, Ella."

"Don't place any bets on that," I snapped, then closed my mouth. *Brain, please keep up.* "I'm sorry. You didn't earn that."

" Maybe I did." He surveyed me, topping a short finger of clear liquid into my cup. "Take it easy, okay?"

I bit back the retort that flowed too fast onto my tongue; it still stung that he'd been right. I hadn't changed. Even after ten years, that same girl was hidden beneath my bravado, the same love-struck one who dumped him and walked away carrying her own shattered heart.

I blinked back memories far too close to the surface and cast about for a much safer topic. "Does the storm look any closer?"

Andy turned to look at me fully, the corner of his lips quirked.

Weather? I'm talking to him about the weather? Kill me now.

To his credit, Andy didn't laugh. "It's closing in. We might be stuck here for a bit."

I eyed him suspiciously. "How long is a *bit?*"

"Maybe a day, maybe more." His eyes drifted the length of me, lingering on my side. I placed my hand over the bandage.

"No. You don't get to use my injury as a reason to keep me cooped up."

Andy snorted. "Same old Ella, huh?" His eyes held a definite sparkle this time. "What makes you think I'd want to stay cooped up with the girl who broke my heart?"

His hand tightened on my ankle for a moment, then lightened, making little circles around the bone. I held back a small moan; he'd always had a thing about my legs, and his touch was magic. As he stroked the arch of my very bare feet, it belatedly occurred to my fuzzy brain that he'd half undressed me, removing my shoes and socks and half of my shirt.

My lips twitched while I pretended not to think about it. "Oh, something about a witty conversation, great company, rekindling an old flame..." I bit my lip.

That last one slipped out. I chose to blame the alcohol, though I suspected there was far too much truth in it. Being so close to him again was doing odd things to my heart, and my mind struggled to catch up.

Andy stared into the dancing flames, his hands tracing intricate patterns around my ankles, sliding just inside the hem of my jeans. I sighed, slipping back down a little into my blankets. My eyes drifted closed, and I let the warmth of his comfort wash over me.

CHAPTER ELEVEN

ANDY

I watched her sleep. Small worry lines formed around her eyes and crinkled her brow disappeared as Ella rested. Sleep allowed her to relax beneath the stresses of being chased, the shock of her injury, and the added influence of alcohol.

Slipping the glass from between her hands, I placed it next to mine on the coffee table that sat beside the sofa. My handgun rested beside it, close enough that I could grab if anyone battered their way through the door.

Ella's feet rested on my legs. I went back to massaging them even though she wouldn't notice. I'd spent a year holding her, touching her. Loving her.

And ten times the same, missing her like hell.

That she'd broken her own heart alongside mine to give me the career I'd chased still blew me away. Maybe I hadn't been clear enough that I wanted — *needed?* — her with me. It was so long ago, with so many emotions packed into that decade-long block. I couldn't spend the night going back over those when I had the perfect woman sleeping across my lap.

Ella had always been generous. With her love, her time, or anything she had to offer. Which was plenty. And if she'd changed, I barely saw it — underneath, she still buzzed with passion and energy, believing in everyone.

Everyone but herself.

My lips curled up.

She'd managed to pull together a career and business — no easy task for a girl who refused to try for college, swearing she wasn't smart enough.

Others might see her self-doubt as a weakness, but I saw it as a sign of her inner strength.

Wind rattled the door, picking up pace outside. When I'd collected the firewood from the small back porch, I'd scanned the woods behind the place for signs of movements, but nothing — apart from the local wildlife — had sprung up.

I kept an ear out for the men who'd chased her. Yet, I was pretty certain they would have returned to collect their motorbikes at the homestead by now, neither determined nor stupid enough to brave the snow closing in on the mountain.

Chances were that we would be able to stay warm inside the cabin safely for tonight, but tomorrow we'd have to make the hike back, for medical attention for Ella, if nothing else. Tequila was a good thing, but not with a lack of food. I'd checked the cupboards and had been surprised at the lack of canned stock, considering Bill must have cut the firewood only this last season.

Maybe after he'd fallen ill, Maise had come to collect them all. *Dying of a broken heart*, Ella had said.

My own chest tightened. I took a deep breath to loosen it, shrugging the thought away. I was concerned with how I'd get Ella back down the mountain with a sore side and an empty stomach.

Tomorrow would bring pain for her, I knew. The second day was always the worst, and that old adage didn't just apply to the gym. Settling back, I watched the flames, letting them mesmerize me. The feel of her beneath my hands, the lithe muscle curving as she arched beneath me, the sandalwood scent of her skin mixed with something floral she washed with remained with me, ten years on.

It didn't take long for the sweet images to be replaced with something more sensual. My mind watched her ride me, cowgirl style. For all the time we'd spent in each other's arms, we'd never actually fallen asleep or woken up together — the joys of a high school relationship. I grinned at the flames, watching them dance, recalling the feel of her.

My arousal grew until I could almost feel her beneath my hands, pressing her onto my hips. I dashed the thought away. It clung to me, anyway. Shifting uncomfortably, I tried to distract myself with work.

Fail, Andy.

And just like that, I needed her as badly as I always had.

What sort of a Ranger are you?

A damned shit one.

I clenched my teeth, slugging back the remaining tequila. It coursed a vicious path through my veins, its effects dulled by the need that overwhelmed me.

I shook my head and went back to brooding before the fire. The glow reminded me of the neon santas across from my office. Counting back, I realised Ella had been right. I was shit with dates. I'd lost a few days over work and totally forgotten that it

136

was Christmas Eve, what with chasing Ella up a mountain.

I snorted; it suited the mood. Blinking tired eyes, I had to admit to myself how exhausted I was, as well. The empty glass listed in my hand. Fatigued muscles spasmed, then loosened in my back.

My energy seeped away in the safety of the cabin, and I hoped to God I wasn't wrong about the men who had shot at Ella turning back to the homestead.

Covering a yawn with the back of my hand, I glanced at my watch. It was only eight in the evening, though it felt much later, and I settled back to rest my eyes.

Less than a moment later, hairs rose beneath my shirt. I swiveled upright from my slump, both ankles and knees protesting from being in the same position for so long as I caught her minute movement.

Ella stared at me with eyes clear of pain. She blinked, her steady gaze trained on me, hyper-aware.
I reached for her cautiously, lest I raise the beast. "How are you feeling?"

"I'm fine." Her voice gravelly from sleep did nothing to ease my aroused state.

I imagined waking up next to her and the far more explicit fantasy that had come after. My eyes traveled the length of her dark-denim-clad legs, my hands clenching with the need to peel them off her, and lick every inch of the skin exposed that came after.

"You should have water." I shook myself mentally, hardly willing to allow her to see how she affected me after all this time when she clearly didn't want me.

No matter how my heart protested to the contrary, I couldn't deny that even though she'd admitted she hadn't wanted to leave me in the first place, she'd blacklisted me and never made any attempt to find me afterward.

It was just a chance, silly season meeting. That was all.

I am a damned Texas Ranger.

And who gave that extra push when you doubted it? Who believed in you when you didn't?

She raised herself up in a stunted, jerky movement, shifting her elbows behind her. Her chest flared out, she stretched as much as her injury allowed, but after a moment, her eyes blinked closed.

I stared at the curve of her breasts that made my groin ache.

Opening her eyes, she licked her lips. "Is there a bathroom?"

"One in the back, fully equipped. Let me—" I slipped my arms beneath her, unraveling the remaining blankets.

She bent, wincing, but made not a single sound.

My hand brushed her back, sending a tiny electric shock through me.

"Thanks, Andy," she said, swiping a hand across tired eyes. My arms hovering around her for support she didn't need, I led her across the small room to the even smaller bathroom.

"I'll get you some water." I collected her glass and strode to the small kitchenette, filling it too far. I took a sip, reminding myself to back away from the ex-girlfriend as my brain cells blessedly kicked in.

Collecting a fresh dressing, tape, and disinfectant she'd likely squall about, I headed back across the room that was suddenly far too confined.

Some part of me was glad she was injured, though not because she was hurt, but because it limited the contact we could have.

From the woman I'd fantasized about for years.

Smooth, Andy.

She was faster than I'd expected, and back on the sofa within a few minutes, wrapped in the nest of blankets. A little shiver passed over her as she shifted.

My teeth clenched in sympathy. What I wouldn't give for a few painkillers right now for her. Or a doctor.

I took a step closer, proffering the glass. Ella leaned forward, taking a sip, her eyes on me the whole time.

I swallowed, so hard it was painful.

My hips moved to adjust myself through my jeans without using my hands, holding her gaze.

Her chest rose and fell in a long rhythm, and I wondered how long she'd been watching me, her gaze holding no sign of drowsiness.

"Ella—" I cleared my throat, "I'd like to check your dressing. Please."

Keep it on a professional front. Keep it easy.

Without breaking eye contact with me, she reached down, her slim fingers curling beneath the hem of her shirt, drawing it slowly upwards. The material lifted higher, past the dressing, exposing a

140

taut stomach I'd tried hard not to look at and failed when I was tending her injury.

She's a wounded girl, buddy. Back the fuck away. Now.

I knelt beside the sofa, taking the glass she offered back, empty.

"Good girl," I murmured.

"Always."

Lost in her eyes, I forced myself to drag my gaze away from her face and down her body to her wound. Her hands fell away as I lifted mine. "May I?"

"Go ahead."

Every word that fell from her lips was an invitation. I squared my mind back on the job and only succeeded in frustrating myself more.

Her stomach was the same tight muscle beneath gorgeous, honey-colored skin. I convinced myself that holding her other side was necessary in my need to check a dressing that shouldn't have been touched after the first round. I cautiously peeled back the tape, seeing nothing but fresh, pink flesh.

No longer weeping, I was glad the wound didn't have any infection obvious to the naked eye. No stripes of red flared outward from the injury that was thankfully more a deep graze than a puncture. However, tomorrow would tell how well I'd treated it, or if I'd missed anything embedded in her flesh.

I laid the original dressing back, pressing the tape down gently. It didn't stick quite as well as it had before. I frowned.

"What is it?"

"I'm glad I brought extra supplies over." I waved the disinfectant and gauze.

"And what do you think you're going to do with that?" she asked tartly.

"I'm going to fix this."

I bent over my task, setting the new tape, dressing, and disinfectant on my knee.

Ella pressed up, peering at me. "Are you fucking kidding, Andy?"

"What? I want to make sure this is clean and ready for tomorrow." I focused on my preparations for getting her down that treacherous hillside.

"There's more than one way to make me scream, Andy."

I stopped.

In fact, the whole world stopped. I wasn't sure if it was her using my name, or my imagination. Need. Looking into her eyes, I could see she meant it. Not the pain, but that her longing mirrored mine.

142

"*Jesus Christ*, Ella," I swore, dolloping a slug of tequila into her glass. I downed and replaced it, knowing it was on an empty stomach for both of us. "Drink that, or pour it on your injury."

"I'm not wasting that on the wound," she protested, taking the shot from me with a surprisingly steady hand. She tipped it back and held it out for a refill. "Use the lemon and salt on it if you have to."

"Could you die a more horrible death?" I topped her off against my better judgement, which was screaming behind a solid wall of broken sensibilities. I'd prefer to hide from it, for now. Especially with the woman I loved spread out before me. As she dashed the shot back, I poured disinfectant on a fresh fold of bandage. I pressed it over the top of the old one, letting it seep down onto the wound, fussing unnecessarily.

Ella reared up, swallowing the tequila first, thankfully. Most of it. A ragged breath hissed from her lips, her chest heaving.

"Careful, you'll drown me." I gave her a grin, wiping a fine mist from my arm.

"Remind me never to let you do triage on a farm. Or a battlefield," she wheezed, waving my hand away. "Wow. Is it meant to go numb?" Her fingers probed her side then drifted back to her lips, echoing the same movement.

My eyes narrowed. "Your mouth or your side is numb?"

Ella pressed her tongue to her lips in a mesmerizing movement.

I followed the tip of pink as it prodded her lip, then slid between them as she squeezed her hand over mine. Testing.

"Um. Either? "Her hand covered mine over her wound then beneath, trying to slide her fingers under mine, but I wasn't having a bar of it.

"Nu-uh. I don't trust you to hold compression tight enough." I taped the fresh bandage on top of the old one and grasped the hem of her shirt, fingering the edge of the material. I was torn between pressing it back and being the gentleman — *the Ranger* — and desperately wanting to rip it apart, lay her bare before me, and hear those screams I remembered her making with clarity as I administered to her with my mouth.

Her mouth widened in a perfect 'o'. "You don't trust me?"

"Not in this." I snorted, gathering what little control I had, leaning back. "Put your outrage away, baby. Have another shot."

144

I shouldn't have, but I did, pouring with my free hand. The fingers of my other hand slid across her stomach, tracing curves I'd spent too many nights dreaming about. Her chest rose slowly, plump lips parted as she stared at me with heavy eyes.

My heart clenched, praying I wasn't pushing her. But the gentleman in me had taken a vacation, the need of having her beneath me again taking over.

CHAPTER TWELVE

ELLA

Andy's touch burned a path far more searing than the tequila across my skin, proving that everything was not numb, after all. Memories of our first kisses whirled in my head — in the school gym when we'd waited until everyone had left for the day, when he walked me home.

But those had been innocent touches, at least at first until we'd become more exploratory. The intensity of his gaze on me promised me nothing so sweet.

I pressed my thighs together, clenching against the sudden spurt of need that had been growing since he sat down. I hoped he missed the movement as he passed my glass back.

"Thank you," I whispered, my throat closing in tight.

Why would he want me again after all this time? The feel of him rubbing my feet dragged up nights watching sports together — well, him watching, me reading, or sketching designs that were never made into anything. Or dozing. His hands running up my legs and peeling my jeans off me afterward, his mouth—

I squeezed my eyes closed for a quick second, not wanting to go there. Especially if there was no chance of feeling his hands on me like that ever again. Which I desperately wanted.

I turned the glass in my hands. Maybe my perception *was* a little skewed.

Andy had always been so easy to get along with, to relax beside.

When I'd walked away from him the first time, it had created an enormous rift deep inside me. I'd tried desperately to fill it, first with my own business, then with looking after my family. No matter how I distracted myself, the gap was still there; just a few tentative band-aid fixes stuffed over the top in the hope of concealing the damage beneath.

The logical part of my brain stated facts while my heart went into overdrive.

Andy's fingers curled around my uninjured side, his fingertips curving beneath me to stroke my spine.

My breath hitched in response then stopped completely.

"Andy," I whispered, swallowing a terrifying blend of fear and desire. He held my gaze, the sparkle in them deepening into a dark blaze. My stomach tightened, and I knew he felt my reaction to him. "I—"

But the words got stuck somewhere between my lungs and my mouth. Possibly as I was out of breath.

Andy slid me along the sofa over his legs, taking exquisite care with my sore side. Not that I could feel it anyway, but I appreciated the care he took, as he had always done.

I clung to his arms, my heart accelerating to a panic point as he shifted the pillows beneath me. Maybe I was imagining this? Maybe—

He leaned into me, bracing his arms over my head. The leathery scent of him washed over me, mixing with his own brand of salty sweat to create an intoxicating cloud around me. I shifted as his legs pressed against mine, sliding my knees apart.

My god, I'm almost panting, and he hasn't even kissed me yet.

Lifting me against him, he settled his weight carefully over me. The familiar feel of his doused my senses, my body shifting to accommodate him. His hips flexed between

149

my legs, against the center of me, and I couldn't hold back a small gasp.

"Am I hurting you?" Concern etched his eyes.

"Andy, if you don't kiss me, I'm going to jump you."

The corner of his mouth lifted, but his eyes were hooded. "I'd like to see that."

Before I could retort, he caught my jaw between firm fingers, tilting my head back to expose my throat. His lips brushed the most sensitive of spots he'd always known how to find, his teeth grazing the sensitive dip where my neck met my shoulder.

I whimpered, attempting not to writhe beneath him.

He laughed against my skin, mouth pressed over my erratic pulse. His tongue flicked against it in time. "I *do* still know you, Ella," he said in a low voice, driving a bolt of desire straight through me.

I threaded one hand through his hair, my other curling around his shoulder. It filled my hand with a familiar shape, though his muscles were harder than before, more defined.

Peppering my jaw with tiny kisses, he slid his knee between my legs so slowly that I twisted beneath him.

"I'm not going to break."

"You can't feel the pain," he replied, completely reasonable.

"I can feel you." I wrinkled my nose as he pulled back. "Don't you dare—" Winding my hands back into his hair, I drew him back to me, encountering little resistance as he dipped his mouth to mine.

Our lips brushed once, twice, pausing a breath apart.

His eyes hooded, he drew a deep breath in. Andy's mouth pressed against mine for a single second, then our lips crashed together as memory and reality merged. His arms wound around me, cradling me against the warmth of him, enveloping my body with his.

I arched against him as his tongue swept inside my mouth, needing to get closer. Moaning at the familiar taste of him, the controlled need in him uncoiling, I tried to feel everything and remember everything about him at the same time. A sensory overload swept over me, resulting in a deep moan that tore from my lips.

Andy groaned in a soft echo of my desire, his hands sweeping along my body as if trying to memorize it all at the same time.

My fingers slipped each button of his shirt free. He lifted his chest, shucking the cotton away without breaking contact with my mouth. His kisses became brutal, demanding as I wound myself against him, my hands sliding over musculature that definitely hadn't been that defined before.

The sofa moved beneath me. I blinked against something pink and fluffy that tickled my cheek. My heart hammering, I broke the kiss.

"Are you okay?" Andy tucked his hands around me.

"What happened?" I blinked again as his mouth dragged over mine again.

"We fell off the sofa. I think," he mumbled against my skin. "Do you hurt?"

I shook my head, trying to bring his mouth back to mine. "Not the way you mean."

He drew back, the dark flame in his eyes ablaze with lust, promising me wicked things.

I dragged my fingers lightly over each new rise and curve of muscle that carved his incredible physique, tracing the vee of his hips to where it disappeared into the top of his jeans. With a hiss, he caught my hands in his, bringing them back to my chest.

"Take it slow, babe. I need to find you again."

"I think you already have."

His sinful smile said everything he didn't as his mouth descended on mine again. Every kiss stole my breath, my heart racing as his hands found every curve, traced every sensitive place on my body.

I loved rediscovering every inch of him, finding the hardened sinew beneath the shapes I knew so well.

He tore his mouth from mine, and he untied the neckline of my shirt, flicking the tiny buttons apart until the flimsy material lay on either side of me. His mouth trailed the tops of my breasts, his fingers nimbly flicking open the clasp at the front, and my bra joined the pile of material.

I stared up at him, my hands halting in their own tour as his thumbs grazed the sides of my breasts, just beneath their swell. I curled my hands around his back, and moaned my need, tiny gasps drawn from my lips with his every touch.

By the time his circling fingertips and tongue touched my aching nipples, the buds so tight with arousal, I could have screamed. When he nipped one lightly, pinching the other at the same time, I *did* scream, curling my nails into his shoulders.

"Fuck, Ella," he growled, running his fingers between my legs. I whimpered, my breath coming too fast. He tugged at the button of my jeans. "God, girl, are you sure? I don't want to hurt you—"

"You won't," I whispered, not caring if I was begging. "Please, Andy."

That was all it took, for both of us.

He peeled my jeans away with the same care he'd taken earlier, taking my white lace panties with them. Andy exhibited far more control than I could muster, trying to kick them free with little grace, ignoring the numbed pull at my side. He sent me an amused glance, trailing kisses along my legs, pausing to nip gently at the inside of my knees.

Andy rose to remove his own jeans, unbuckling his belt with his eyes on me the entire time. It may have been the sexiest sight I'd had in person for far too long. Naked and stretched out on the floor beneath him, I should have felt vulnerable, but I didn't.

I traced the lines of his body with my eyes as his jeans bunched on the floor at his feet. Lines of muscle more defined than I remembered shaped his ripped body. Those broad shoulders I'd adored as a teen were built just that little bit extra, every inch of him tanned from the waist up.

And from the waist below...well, I already knew I wouldn't be disappointed there.

Andy knelt between my legs, leaning in to kiss me. He left me breathless as he drew a scorching path from my mouth to my stomach, kissing tenderly around the bandage.

I wiggled in protest.

"Easy, babe. I don't remember you being this impatient."

"It's been ten years, Andy," I huffed. My head finally caught up with my mouth, and I squeezed my eyes shut for an instant.

Andy's kisses stopped, and I knew he'd seen it.

He sat up straight, hands curling around my thighs. "What?" He stared at me, his eyes widening. "Are you saying..."

I turned my head to study the fire, still burning steadily, and didn't answer him. My stomach clenched, and I knew I shouldn't have said anything, but the tequila seemed to have extra side effects.

His fingers cupped my cheek, turning my face to his, but I studied his chest instead.

"Ella. Look at me," he commanded, but I ignored him, and shook my head. His fingers slipped over my lips in a gentle caress. "Please?"

"No. I– I haven't been with anyone else since you." I finally looked at him.

Surprise widened his eyes, then they filled with something else. I watched emotions play across his face, and settle in his eyes. Lost in them, it took me a moment to recognize it as wonder.

"You're incredible," he murmured, dipping his head to kiss me deeply, cradling my head, his fingers tangled in my hair. By the time he released me, I was dizzy. "I love you, Ella."

My eyes snapped open.

"What?" I blinked at him, owlishly.

"You heard me," he laughed.

"No, I heard a maniac say something crazy." I tried to lever myself up on my elbows, but my side protested. I lay back with a small gasp.

156

"Careful." He kissed my mouth, then my side, his hands sliding over my hips. "Relax, Ella. It's nothing we haven't done before. I promise I'll take care of you." He raised his head, those azure eyes glowing with tenderness.

The little bit of my heart that had been holding firm to its resolve broke.

"Okay," I whispered.

"Okay? You're sure, Ella? I can stop."

"Don't you dare, Andy Matthews."

He laughed against my stomach, continuing his trail along the length of my body. His kisses and nips at the tops of my thighs drew groans of frustration that rose to satisfied squeaks as he laved over sensitive flesh.

He slipped his hands beneath my ass, sliding my legs over his shoulders.

Desire overran numbed fears, compiling into a list in my head. I ignored them all, but trembled at his touch all the same.

Andy clasped my hand tight for a moment, squeezing. His mouth trailed along the insides of my thighs, licking and flicking until I wriggled beneath his hands.

"Andy," I shifted as much as his hold on me allowed, "*please.*"

157

He paused.

I froze, wondering if I'd whined too much.

His tongue flicked against me, tasting. Large, calloused hands tightening on my ass, he drew me apart, placing those same damned kisses along the length of me, pausing to nip at my clit.

I yelped at the mixture of pleasure and pain, knotting my fingers in the rug beneath me.

"Fuck, I need to hear you do that again," he growled, his tongue flicking against my clit in a rhythm that built quickly.

I moaned, not caring what I sounded like any longer.

His hand found mine again, gripping tight. I clutched at the tether he offered as my orgasm rushed over me, digging my toes into his back.

I sank back into the rug with a whimper, begging for more, but satisfied beyond measure, and he released my hand. His tongue explored, stroking along my folds and back, making a pathway around my most sensitive flesh. Tracing over that same area, he slid a finger deep inside me, mirroring the rhythm of his tongue. I whimpered, the pleasure building again, so fast.

He slid a second finger in very slowly, pressing hard inside me.

I arched at the overwhelming sensations, wrapping my legs around his shoulders. Smiling against my skin, he nipped my clit again, and I screamed, white-hot pleasure ripping through me.

Warm arms surrounded me. I opened my eyes lazily, trying to shift, but the effort was monumental. The arm around my tight end as he stroked gently over my clit and back again. I shivered with the aftershocks of my orgasm — *had there been more than one?*— arching back to kiss him. Tasting myself on his lips sent a smaller shock over me.

Andy drew back. "Are you okay? Did I hurt you?"

I shook my head, not trusting myself to speak. Tilting my head back, I strained to kiss him again, needing him closer, everywhere.

His mouth came down on mine again. Harder, wilder, demanding.

I gasped against his lips, his tongue dancing with mine, his hands tangling in my hair as he moved around me. Sensation Stumbled over me, his movements too fast for my mind to process everything at one.

159

Mewls tore from my lips as he pressed me back, Andy kissed along my neck, sliding his knees between mine.

"Wait– I want to—"

"Tonight is for you. Just you." He kissed my eyelids, the corners of my mouth. "Give me time to prove I've missed you for the last ten years, Ella. So damn much. I tried to fill the gap you left but it broke me. Let me give tonight to you, and you can have every night after for whatever you want."

Capturing my hand in his, he guided my fingers to wrap around his cock. I kept my touch light, remembering him, and watched his eyes, gauging every touch. Brushing my palm over the tip of him earned me a deep, shuddering breath.

I slid my hand all the way around him, finding a rhythm his hips reacted to. Breath hissing between his teeth, he gripped my hand tight again, guiding himself to my entrance.

I shifted my hips a little, getting used to the feel of him there. I was torn between the urge to slide him all the way into me or to take it slowly at the damning pace he seemed to prefer.

His fingers clasped around mine, he drew our hands to his mouth, kissing my knuckles.

"Tell me if I need to stop, Ella."

"I will not tell you anything of th—"

Andy's mouth came down on mine, opening my lips with his tongue as he slid inside me. The world exploded around us, or stilled. I couldn't tell the difference.

My moan slipped into his mouth as I tried to buck against him, but his hand on my hips held me still.

He filled me an inch at a time, pausing halfway. "Is this okay?"

I fixed him with a hard stare, clenching around him tight to draw a soft groan from him that sent a rush of heat tearing through me.

"If you ask me one more time, I'll—"

He slid the rest of the way inside me with a single motion, stealing my breath, though I would have screamed if I could. My eyes flung opened, not knowing I'd closed them. I drowned, caught in his hooded, midnight-dark gaze.

Andy moved slowly, pausing at the top of each movement only to bury himself deep within me in the next.

My breath mixed with desperate cries as I drew him down to me. Tangling my arms and legs around his, I matched his thrusts as much as his hand on my hip allowed. My knees pressed against his back, trembling as my orgasm tore through me. His thrusts erratic, he held on for a second more before he roared, arching over me, his breath hot on my throat as he slammed into me a final time.

Throbbing, my limbs tightened around him, never wanting to let this perfect man go, ever again.

CHAPTER THIRTEEN

ANDY

Firelight flickered over her perfect body curled into mine, marred only by the bandage on her side, hidden between us. I hooked my toe around a blanket folded neatly beside the sofa, flicking it up over both of us.

No sound came from outside, and I knew the snow had fallen heavy, blanketing the forest around us. Whatever the damage, we had missed the worst of it, wrapped in each other. Paired with the snow, it was a protection of sorts.

Ella had fallen asleep within moments, curling into my shoulder as I rolled to face the fire, careful of her side. God knew what that would feel like in the morning when the tequila wore off, but for now, she was resting.

I brushed a wayward strand of auburn hair from her skin, glowing gold beneath the flames.

"How did I get so lucky?" I murmured, kissing her forehead.

"You have no idea the level of crazy that comes with me." She nestled deeper into my chest with a kitten-soft yawn.

"I thought you were asleep."

"I was," her voice was muffled against my chest, "and I'm going back there right now."

"Are you?" I dipped my mouth to where her neck curved, brushing my lips over her tender skin there. She shivered. Hell, I needed her again already. "Are you hurting?"

She was silent for a moment, and my heart stopped.

Had I pushed this on her? I held my breath, my lips barely contacting her skin.

"No," she whispered, raising her good arm to hook behind my head, pressing down gently.

"Good," I growled, nipping her neck lightly, teasingly. Testing her.

She cried out, arching against me, and I hardened instantly, desperate to sink myself deep into her. I pressed one arm the length of her, holding her back against me, my other hand splayed between her breasts.

To feel her reaction to my touch was almost too much. I reigned in my control on a tight wire as I traced the shape of her breasts with my mouth, arching over her as I nudged her thighs apart with my knee. She moaned, my cock settling against the curve of her ass, between her cheeks. I pulled her back to me, still cautious of her wound, but a little harder, nonetheless.

Ella tilted her head back, her mouth searching for mine as her hand behind my neck drew me down to her. Her tongue stroked mine in a dance filled with desire and need, just as demanding as I had been before.

I curled my hand around the inside of her leg, brushing lightly over the soft, pale flesh of her inner thigh.

She rewarded me with a shiver, her hands trembling over mine. A tiny moan built in her throat.

I smiled against her skin, rubbing myself against that rounded ass. My fingers drifted to the core of her, finding her drenched with both our fluids. I made a trail from her clit and back, my other hand holding her back against my chest as she whimpered, writhing in place. Her hand wrapped around my wrist, tugging. I ignored her, sliding two fingers deep inside her.

She arched, her head thrown back over my shoulder, auburn hair falling away to expose her throat. I nipped her in the same place as before, pressing my lips and tongue to the spot to soothe the instant pain. She cried out, gripping my wrists tight in her smaller hands, trusting me to hold her up.

Smiling, I curled both fingers inside her, nipping her neck a little harder.

Ella screamed, stretched taut as her orgasm spiraled over her, clenching hard on my fingers. Her hips still rocking with the violence of her orgasm, I didn't wait for her to stop, catching her thigh. My hand coated with her pleasure, I stroked her soft flesh and slid inside her.

Her breath coming in fast, shallow pants, she clenched around me, her hips bucking. Raw moans that ripped from her throat nearly sent me over the edge. I'd intended to love her sweetly, but something far more primal flooded through me. I needed this woman, needed to know she was mine again and that I would have her next to me every day, to wake up to her every morning for the rest of my life.

Her cry morphed into a moan that rocked me as the last of her resistance failed and she sank back into me, bone deep.

I inhaled sharply through my nose, willing myself not to come yet. Gripping her uninjured hip firmly, I slid almost all the way out, fucking her gently for fear of hurting her. A steady stream of whimpers tore from her mouth, her hand still wrapped tight around my wrist.

"Andy, please— I need you to—"

"Shh, babe, let me love you." I kissed her mouth, and she sighed beneath the gentle pressure, her whole body shuddering as tremors and aftershocks collided.

Ella pushed back against me, and I let myself sink deeper into her, immersed in her. She clenched tight around me, and I slid my fingertips over her clit, brushing back and forth as she came again.

Her hips curved gently beneath my hand as I thrust into her deeper, gauging her cries. Her legs curled around mine, her feet sliding the length of my calf. She wrapped her fingers around my thigh, pulling me deeper.

My control failed. I gripped her tight, arching as my own pleasure rolled over me, leaving me coiled around her.

Ella slumped against my chest within the confines of my arms, breathing heavily. I made patterns over her shoulder, tasting the saltiness of her. Both of us were slick with sweat. She hadn't moved, and I was content to stay inside her, unwilling to break the smallest contact with her.

She mumbled something against my arms. I shifted, moving my shoulder beneath her head.

"I've got you." I tightened my arms around her, waiting until her breath evened, slowing.

Resting my head on the hideous pink rug in the cabin that used to be a Rangers Hut, I settled around her, wondering how in the hell we would get down the mountain come morning.

❖

I woke with aching shoulders and something tickling my ribs. Raising a head that throbbed with a headache that came more from sleeping on the floor than from imbibing tequila, I squinted at Ella as she made her way down my body.

"What are you doing? And aren't you hurt?"

She smiled, moving her mouth over my ribs. Tiny kisses were interspaced with flicks of her tongue, and I remembered vividly just what she could do with that mouth.

I groaned at the thought, hardening again as her hand drifted over my skin, stroking lightly, almost painfully gentle in her touch. I caught her shoulder, and she raised her head, the glazed stare in her eyes gave me pause.

Gripping her arms, I drew her slowly along me, then pressed her back to the floor. Barely making a noise, she settled on the rug, her honey dark eyes drifting closed without a fuss.

"Ella? Baby, open your eyes for me. Ella?" I pressed a hand to her forehead, swearing at the heat flaming there.

Her bandaged area looked fine. I gently tugged back the oversized bandage to check. The wound itself looked clean — red and puffy, but what bothered me were the red stripes flaring outward from the edges.

Slipping out from under the rug, I left the blanket covering her, grabbing my jeans on my way to the cabinet I'd found the first

169

aid supplies in before. I searched through it, knowing there was nothing to help with pain or fever there, but I checked anyway, cursing under my breath.

I pressed my hands to the countertop, noting how cold it was. Swearing again, I found my shirt and relit the fire, stoking it back to life. Although she was hot now, if I let Ella get cold, she could suffer worse.

Undressing her had been simple at the time, but putting those clothes back on a body that was floppy and semi-conscious was a whole new level of difficulty. Managing not to injure her father was another matter.

Finally getting her jeans on, I eased Ella back onto the lounge, arranging pillows and blankets as best I could around her, and went to hunt for something to make into a cold compress.

A new bandage appeared to be my best option, though I also discovered a ready supply of instant coffee and long-life milk. It might be tough, but for today, I'd deal with it.

Armed with a full mug and the compress, I made my way back to the sofa, surprised to see Ella sitting up and almost alert. I perched on the edge of her pillow nest, not wanting to irritate her wound further, especially with such a likelihood of infection.

"How are you feeling?" I asked cautiously. She liberated my coffee, drawing it close to her. I pressed my hand to her forehead. Still hot, but not flaming like it had been a few minutes ago. That worried me more — I definitely needed to get her to a doctor soon. Now. I grinned to cover my worry. "Did you wake up because I made coffee?"

"Mhmm." She took a long sip. "Thank you."
"That was mine, actually. You were– unconscious. I think." Doubt seeded with the worry, but I pushed it aside. "We need to get you home."

Ella studied me with dark hazel eyes. "Merry Christmas."

"Hell, I completely forgot that. Dates, huh? Merry Christmas, Ella." I leaned over the coffee, lacing my fingers through her hair, and kissed her soundly.

When I drew back, her eyes were still half-closed, dozy. But clear, not like her fever-ridden stare from earlier. That had to be a good thing.

171

"We drank too much tequila last night," she stated.

I gave her a wide grin, rubbing the back of my neck. "Yeah. Probably. But still..." I brushed my fingers over her cheek.

She fixed me with a steady gaze, and for a moment, I was back in training, about to be tested. "Did you mean what you said last night?"

"Which bit?" I asked.

The words fell out of my mouth with little thought, and she looked away. My mind caught up seconds too late.

I scrambled to regain the ground I'd lost, reaching for her shoulders to square her off to me so I could look right into her eyes when I said it. Thankfully, she didn't flinch or move away this time.

"Ella. I love you," I said the words carefully, clearly, wanting no discrepancies between us. She blinked once, and said nothing. "I don't think I ever stopped. When you left, I—" I scrubbed my hand over the back of my neck again, creating a sore spot. "I nearly didn't go through with training. Without you there— it was my idea to join the Rangers, but you helped me believe I could do it, especially with a..."

I let the sentence die with a one-shouldered shrug.

"With a family reputation like yours to live up to," she finished for me softly.

"Something like that."

A head of auburn hair accosted me at chin height. I rocked back with the force of her arms wrapping around my ribs.

"I loveyoutoo." Her words ran together, muffled by my chest.

Holding back a grin that threatened to take over my face, I slid my hand between us, catching her chin. I lifted her face to mine, dipping my head so our mouths almost touched.

"Say it again."

"I love you, Andy Matthews." Her eyes shone with her words. She gave me a little shove. "But I would still break up with you. Before. To save you."

"I didn't need saving, Ella. I needed you."

"Mmmphmm." She gave me a half-grin.

"You don't believe me?" I laughed, draining the coffee. A shiver ran over her. She swatted the hand I placed on her forehead. "You're not hot."

"Gee, thanks."

173

"No, I mean, you don't have a fever anymore."

"I'm *cold*, Andy."

"Ahh." I checked the fireplace. The small fire I had created earlier had burned through, and I had no more kindling. I grimaced, knowing I had to go back outside. "I'll get more wood."

I buttoned up my shirt quickly, shoving my feet into my boots. Although it was probably stunning outside in the pristine morning snow — *a white Christmas after all, how 'bout that?* — I wasn't prepared to freeze my ass off for its beauty. I took a breath and opened the door.

A dark shirt blocked my way, all too recognizable.

"Jesus, Henderson. You scared the shit out of me. Glad you came to get us, though." I gestured to Ella on the sofa behind me.

The Ranger smiled, his eyes leaving my face for a moment. I followed his downward glance to the gun in his hand.

An opponent will tell you their next move with their eyes. It's the only place you need to look.

Archer had said that when I first walked into his office. It had sounded mad then, but his crazy ass advice might have saved my life.

My gaze connected with Henderson's again for the split second it took for my mind to catch up before he fired, but I wasn't there to be a target.

I hit the ground hard, scrabbling for my own pistol by the sofa as his shot rang in my ears.

In the silence that followed, a single, soft sigh broke it.

My fingers connected with the butt of my gun, closing around it. I didn't bother suppressing my rage as I rolled to face Henderson, firing a double-tap into his chest. Not stopping to watch him fall, I scrambled back to where Ella lay in her nest of blankets, pasty and still.

I pressed shaking fingers to her neck, searching for a pulse that seemed non-existent, but I refused to believe it. I *couldn't*. A tortured breath got stuck somewhere between my shoulder blades as I gulped at air that wouldn't go anywhere. For too long a moment, I knew I'd lost her. But as the world shattered around me, a faint pulse batted my fingertips. I sighed with a minute measure of relief, searching for the wound.

The blankets wound in knots around my hands as my movements became more frantic. Over the site of her old injury, my hands came up bloody. Finally, I managed to expose her damaged side, clutching armfuls of blankets.

The bandages that had been white throughout the night were soaked with blood. I put the blankets to good use, pressing down as hard as I dared, trying to staunch the flow. I prayed it was better than it looked.

The quick glance I'd taken burned the image into my mind: the center a red, tattered mess that flared past her side, scraping open her existing wound. The bullet had grazed her, just.

A small hole punctured the back of the sofa beside her.

Relief slammed into me — though her side was a mess, if the bullet hadn't gone through her flesh, then she'd be okay.

Sore, and bleeding, but okay.

My muddled head returned to my shoulders in a rush that rocked me.

I gripped the gun in my other hand, swinging back to where Henderson was laid out on the ground. Blood pooled around him.

There was no one else outside that I could tell from where I crouched over Ella.

Lucky bastard.

I cursed myself as an idiot. If Henderson had brought anyone with him, I'd be dead by now, likely shot in the back while I tended to Ella. Then no one would be able to help her, and we would both be dead.

Ethan would hand my ass to me for it.

Henderson groaned, rocking in his pool of blood. I watched him dispassionately, stretching my leg to kick his gun away.

"Why aren't you dead?"

"Why are you still alive?" he ground out, clutching his shoulder.

"Answer the fucking question."

"Kevlar. Shit stock. Apparently, it's only good for one hit. Not that I'm complaining." Breath hissed between his teeth as he stared at the ceiling.

"From that distance, it should have failed the first time." My lips curled, and I checked my sights. If I pulled the trigger a third time, it would be a headshot.

"Maybe it's better than I expected, then."

"Slide your phone to me, Henderson." I nudged him with my boot, kicking harder when he only moaned senselessly. One of my shots appeared to have punctured his shoulder. I pressed my heel down on it hard, ignoring his yells. "Give me the fucking phone. That kevlar is pretty useless from here, and it doesn't cover your face."

I let the implicit threat sink in.

His head rolled back, bloodshot eyes glaring balefully at me as he slid his phone across the floor.

I took my hand off Ella's wound to call the office, hoping someone would be there. Jenny wouldn't be on the desk today. Fucking Christmas. It was officially my least favorite holiday.

The call rang through. I hit the speaker button, pressing my hand back to the bundle of blankets over Ella. She coughed behind me. My heart gave a leap, but I didn't take my eyes off Henderson. There were no second chances in a scenario like this — especially for him.

Ella moaned, and I had half a mind to shoot Henderson again, just to satisfy my rage. The call picked up, breaking my line of thought.

"What do you *want*, Henderson?" Jake's voice held a note of derision that poured over the rasp of a late night.

"You got a bad hangover happening there, Jake."

"The fuck? Ow." The phone creaked, static assailing my ear. "What are you doing with Henderson? Tell me you didn't have a night of passion? Merry fucking Christmas," he grumped.

"Ah— we had a night, but passion isn't the word I'd use." I eyed Henderson on the floor. He coughed, rolling his eyes. "The prick shot Ella. Get your ass up the mountain behind Kinland Creek."

More swearing. "Where are you? I'll be..." I could hear the mental gears turning as Jake worked out if he was sober enough to drive.

"Get me a chopper to the old Ranger Hut on Blackman's ridge behind Kinland Creek. Henderson must be part of the rustling." I gave voice to the reason I'd been playing with in my head. "That's right, eh?" I kicked Henderson again. He grunted. I took it as confirmation. "He shot at me and got Ella instead. Fucking Christmas." I barked the last in a harsh enough voice that it grated my throat.

179

"Well, shit. Um, yeah, man, I'll be up there. Shit. She okay?"

"She's been fucking shot, Jake. I think it's a graze, but she was already injured. I need medical *now*."

"On it."

Jake kept the line open while he arranged the chopper. I made sure he got the details right. Waiting for a chopper that was on the other side of the mountains while keeping Ella alive and contemplating killing Henderson wasn't my chosen way to spend Christmas day.

"Andy?"

Ella's hand pressed against my lower back. I leaned into her touch to let her know I'd felt her there, not game to take my eyes off the traitor on the floor.

"Alright. You there, Matthews?"

"Sure, as fuck not going anywhere."

"You will be soon. We're coming."

"Good."

"Listen, do you need me to bring anything? Whose phone are you calling from?"

"Jake, get in the damned chopper and—"

"Yeah, yeah, get there. I got you." He ended the call.

180

I nudged the phone onto the sofa with my leg in case I needed the thing again. My gaze returned to the floor.

Henderson's eyes were closed. The blood around him seemed to be a bigger pool than before.

Good. The bastard deserves it.

Maybe I could hurry his path. My fingers flexed around the grip of my gun, steady fingertips brushing over the trigger.

"You never were much of a Ranger, Matthews. No picture on the wall with your Pa."

I clenched my teeth, refusing to rise to his barb. "Why steal cattle, Christian? Ranger pay not good enough for you? Don't like wearing that little star?"

"Doesn't mean the same thing to me as it does to you. You're just a wanna-be in a white hat," he sneered, staring at the ceiling.

"At least I don't walk around looking like a gunslinger from the wild west. Should I call you Sundance? Go on, rob a damned bank while you're at it." I glared at him with distaste.

"Asshole," Henderson spat, his head lolling back as he stared at me. Hatred emanated from every inch of him, his eyes focused on my gun. "You won't. Ever fired a weapon outside a range before today? Ever killed? You couldn't."

"Couldn't I?" My whole body was numb, my nerves marble hard. I wondered if I'd still feel nothing if I pulled the trigger. Again.

The fingers flexed on my back again.

I nodded.

"How are you feeling?" I softened my voice for her, but my words still came out harsh.

The fingers tapped a short rhythm on my back. "It stings a little bit."

I barked a laugh. "Only you would say that, Ella."

"Remember when you told me you were joining the Rangers?"

I blinked, thinking back. The day before my high school graduation. She was a year behind me. And she'd dumped me the day after. I'd planned a big dinner out with her that night, in celebration. The memory soured. "What of it?"

"You glowed, Andy. You'd told your Dad, and you were the happiest I'd ever seen you. Then," she added, and I could hear the smile in her voice, "you were perfect."

"You broke this *perfect* boy's heart," I snapped, wincing.

"You're not a boy anymore. Andy, you need to wait for Jake."

I blinked again, a harsh laugh spitting between my lips. "Always the loyal dog that does what it's told."

There was silence behind me.

"The loyal Ranger who does what is *needed*," she stressed the last word faintly.

Cold air drifted over us, and I was glad to feel it again. To feel anything.

Her hand slipped under mine, pressing down on the wound. "Do what you need to, Andy."

I started at that; choice.

It wasn't something I often thought about, but in the past few years without her, I'd pigeon-holed myself into a career where that wasn't often an option. My fingers flexed around the pistol grip. I left the weapon cocked, ready to fire, but lowered it to aim at the cabin floor well behind Henderson's head.

Behind me, Ella shifted with a gasp to curl her legs around me, getting as much contact from our position as she could.

An hour later, the erratic roar of the chopper's motor reverberated across the

183

valley. Ella nestled against my bare back, her lips pressed to my shoulder. She had barely moved in all that time. But I felt her heartbeat through her shirt, and it reassured me.

Henderson was white in a sea of red, one hand pressed to a bundle of shirt I'd tossed at him for compression, still glaring at me. At least he'd shut up.

It was a long hour, but it wasn't as dark as it might have been.

CHAPTER
FOURTEEN

ELLA

My ears still rang with the whine of the helicopter. Andy refused to let me go the entire time. He'd filled in his workmate Jake — the other Ranger — and cuffed Christian Henderson to a gurney similar to the one I refused. A medic gave me a shot after treating my side, a salty drink with orders to down the lot, a heavy blanket, and left me in Andy's care under the provision she would be called back if anything changed about my condition.

"Jake says Henderson had been hunting around the office, looking for me."

I looked up from my place in the circle of his arms.

Andy stared across the valley, his back to the small cottage.

"I thought he was part of the cattle rustlers," I said, frowning. "He admitted as much, on the cabin floor." I bit my lip before

I could say more. There had been more than one moment when I'd thought Andy would shoot the injured Ranger — again.

"He was."

"Then..?"

"I feel like I'm missing something. Henderson hasn't been around for months, then he all of a sudden he comes poking around my office while my bosses are away." His eyes narrowed. "And he *knew.*" His arms tightened around me. I settled back into my place against his chest, not willing to move until Jake called us over to the chopper.

"How?"

One broad shoulder lifted in a shrug. "It just doesn't sit right with me, Ella. We lost a good Ranger last month. My boss' mentor. He was shot in the line of duty. And now I wonder..." Andy let the sentence hand open.

I slipped my hand into his, weaving our fingers together.

Andy wrapped his arms tight around me until we reached Kinland Creek. The homestead was blanketed in snow. It was a beautiful sight — but so was Andy with his leather jacket over a bare chest. I pressed into his skin, wallowing in the warmth and comfort of him.

Leaving me with promises he'd see me soon and a kiss that had made me blush before the paramedics, he'd collected his pick up for the return journey back to Austin.

For me, it was a short flight. The hospital ward was decorated with a mass of tinsel that winked beneath fluorescent lights. Christmas carols played merrily over the speakers in every hallway.

Nurses and doctors prodded me with half a dozen needles and two drips — one for antibiotics and one for fluids to battle dehydration — and bandaged me until I resembled at least half a mummy. I began to doubt Andy would even recognize me.

By the time the nurses left my room, I was exhausted. My mind kept trying to turn over the events of the past twenty-four hours. I was stunned that was all the time that had passed as exhaustion ran over me. It felt as though my body had held on with every reserve of energy until it had permission to crash.

Which apparently, was now, no matter how long I watched the door for Andy's familiar outline.

Unable to keep my eyes open any longer, I sank into a hard, stuffed pillow that became the comfiest I'd ever laid my head on, and passed out.

———◆◆◆———

Bleeping filled my head. A constant, steady sound that was as annoying as it was loud droning between my ears. But that wasn't what had woken me. I struggled to rise out of the fog of sleep, brushing a hand over my tired eyes that refused to focus and got tangled in my drip cords.

"Urg," I enunciated, trying to pull myself up. Pain shot through my side, reminding me why I was in the hospital at all. I sank back into the comfy pillow that had resumed its overused and lumpy concrete facade.

The world moved, what little of the white ceiling I could see tilting with a whirl. It took me far too long to realize it was the bed moving, not the room. I blinked again, getting a little more focus, this time, and turned my head.

Andy bent over the controls of my bed, concentrating on his task. His hair was mussed, and an evening shadow covered his strong jaw line. Those incredible shoulder still wanted to worship were covered in a white shirt that tucked neatly into blue jeans. I was glad he'd managed to find another shirt after he'd given his other one to Henderson.

I shivered at the thought of the man who'd shot me — who had very nearly killed Andy. Jake had explained quietly in my ear that if the shot had actually hit Andy at that range, the damage would have been horrendous.

I would have lost him.

Again.

The bed jolted, and Andy looked up, catching me watching him.

Heat rose in my cheeks.

"Hey." He smiled, blindingly bright and sexy as hell.

Whatever these drugs were they'd put me on, I was good to keep them.

"Can I keep you, too?" I murmured to myself.

Andy sent me a puzzled look. "You're going to be okay," he told me.

I nodded vigorously, then decided that wasn't the best idea and stopped.

He held up a large coffee in a takeaway cup, and I nodded again. Just once, this time.

"The doctors said as much. I would be in pretty bad shape if you hadn't come looking for me. Thank you." I took the coffee, inhaling deeply. At least now I knew what had woken me.

"Anytime. Actually, no." Andy grimaced, rubbing the back of his neck. "Don't get yourself hurt like that again, ever. Okay?"

He scooted his chair closer to my bed, leaning over me. His cupped my cheeks as he dipped his head to kiss me.

By the time he drew back, I wasn't sure I could remember how to breathe.

"Thank you," I whispered again, tears burning the backs of my eyes. I blinked rapidly. First, I couldn't think; now I was over-emotional.

What the hell is wrong with me?

Andy's fingers brushed my cheek, my lips in a touch so tender it brought on a fresh wave of salt.

I closed my eyes when the tears refused to dissolve, leaning into his hand.

"It'll take some time to work through it, Ella. You've had a hell of a shock — and, just a guess, but I suspect you don't go around getting chased by cattle rustlers and shot at on any normal day, right?" Sapphire blue eyes sparkled at me.

I grinned ruefully, shaking my head with the tiniest movement. "Nope. No Rangering for me, thanks. I'll leave that all up to you."

Andy's hand dropped alongside his smile. "Actually, I've been thinking about that..." He sat back, twisting his hat between his hands.

I flapped at him. "Stop that." He opened his mouth, but I flapped again. "No. Don't you dare throw away a dream you've been working on for a decade, Andy Matthews. A decade I did without you that entire time, so you could have that damned career. I know that man got into your head, but that's no reason for you to quit. I don't remember you that way. At all." I fixed him with a hard stare.

He nodded, smiling just a little. "I've had doubts about it all before, Ella. I'm just not up to the standard."

"Whose standard? Your father's? Grandfather's? Andy, those men were heroes who did amazing things. What the hell makes you think you are any less than them?" My voice rose as I struggled to sit up.

Andy's arms wrapped around me in a huge bear hug. The tears went from a smattering to full-blown cascade as I clung to him.

"I don't think I've ever heard you swear before yesterday." He drew back enough to look at me.

Torn between the desire to slap him and the need to hold him close, I stretched up to kiss him. His mouth met mine again, gentler this time. He brushed his lips over my cheek then back to my lips, leaving them tingling.

I leaned back with little resistance when he gently pressed me back to the lump of concrete behind my head.

"Well, you earned it," I said, grudgingly, struggling to remember what he'd said.

"Mmmm." He tucked a strand of hair behind my ear.

Nurses bustled in, interrupting the moment.

Andy sat back while they attended to me. I watched the younger nurse flirt with him while he handled her barrage of questions on all things Rangering.

Finally, they left, the door closing softly behind them.

"That was interesting?" I hiked an eyebrow in his direction, covering my mouth as I yawned. "Wouldn't you miss that sort of adoration?"

"That's not why I do it." His mouth quirked at the corner.

"So, you're staying?"

"I'll think about it. For you. Get some rest. Doc says you'll be here overnight. I have to go back to work," he sent me an apologetic smile, "but I can take you home. When you're ready. If you want." He rose, tapping his hat on his leg. "Unless you have some—"

"I don't," I said firmly. "I'd love you to be here when I discharge and get all untangled." I waved my drips in the air, earning a soft laugh I knew I would remember all night.

"I'll see you tomorrow," he promised.

"Don't forget to smile." I brushed my hand over his bristled cheek as he leaned in to kiss me again. "You're incredible, Andy. Don't let this break your faith in yourself."

He snorted at that. "Let's talk about you having faith in yourself some time, huh? Merry Christmas, Ella."

193

"Merry Christmas, Andy," I whispered to his back as he left the room, carols filling the hall outside.

Tears blurred my last look at him, but at least these were happy ones.

———◆✕◆———

In the end, it was my brother who collected me and drove me home, cursing the entire time. Andy had word his boss was back from his unscheduled sojourn north — he wouldn't say more than that — sending me apologies and hearts to my text messages. I stared at them in some small semblance of wonder.

How many girls could say they'd been out with Andy Matthews — not once, but then again, ten years later?

I shook my head, realizing my brother was still rattling on. Quickly tiring of his rant, I stared out the window. Half of Texas had been covered in the snowstorm that blew through on Christmas Eve, leaving our part of the state blanketed in glittering white. Already, decorations were being taken down, replaced with *Happy New Year* banners with images of fireworks.

All that lead-up to Christmas, and now it's over, that fast.

Chad dropped me at my door.

I refused to let him come in to "settle" me. I suspected what he was ready to settle in for was a long night talking and a few beers, when all I wanted was to check my flowers, assuming many would be ruined over the time I hadn't tended them, take my happy drugs that gave me a few, blessed pain-free hours, and go to sleep.

It was pure luck that I hadn't had any more deliveries to do when I'd headed out to Kinland Creek. Yesterday morning seemed an age ago. And I needed to call someone about Maise. Mom would know. I flicked off a text, waving to Chad while he still ranted, driving away, glad to be home.

My bed called to me as I lined up my painkillers and antibiotics on the benchtop in my kitchen, my eyes already watering. I didn't bother turning on the lights as I changed into my comfiest long-sleeved nightdress and tumbled into my bed, revoltingly pleased to have my own pillow back.

CHAPTER FIFTEEN

ANDY

I rapped on Ella's door for the third time, then called out. The rows of close-set houses put me on edge. Images of suburban housewives and grannies peering through their lacy curtains gave me the heebeegeebees.

Tapping my hat on my leg, I leaned on the door. It pushed open under my hand. I stared at it for the half second that it took for my brain to go screaming into high gear.

Swearing, I unholstered my gun, cocking it as I entered the house. It was completely dark, though I knew she'd come home hours ago. My stomach clenched, but I pushed all emotion to the back of my mind to deal with later.

Calling out to her and rapping on the door seemed like an idiotic idea in hindsight. Ethan had returned before I was due to pick Ella up, and suddenly I was neck deep in assignments. I'd managed to take him aside for a moment, but his look had stalled me before I could say a thing.

197

"You might have doubts about your abilities, Andy, but you're Ranger blood through and through. I believe the boss is going to set you up for a medal for heading out to the homestead."

I'd stammered my way through declining any sort of public announcement or recognition, realizing with sudden clarity that I simply didn't need the confirmation.

Ethan had let me sit on it for an hour before snowballing me with an inch-thick bundle of paperwork.

Jake had been easier to work with, adding his thin report to the mess that covered my desk. I squinted at the bottom line.

Workplace fantasy. Nookie in the boss's office.

The last word had been crossed out and replaced with *desk.* I winced, promising myself never to enter that office again.

"Are you fucking kidding me, Jake?"

He grinned, his crazy depleted with the vacating silly season. "Nope. Swap for a swap? You weren't meant to haul your ass out to Kinland Creek, either. I'm pretty sure that could go on report, too."

"That's true, but—"

"Hell, they wanna give you a medal," Jake snorted.

"Don't go spreading that around." I covered my face with my hands, speaking through my fingers. "I told Ethan not to say anything."

"Fail there, man. Spectacular fucking fail."

I looked up at Jake, holding his gaze for a minute. Something flickered behind his jovial facade. It wasn't forced, exactly, but I couldn't work out what lay in the shadow of his eyes.

"I can't turn that in to Ethan." I nudged the report with my fingertip as though it was sullying my desk.

Jake's grin got bigger. "You told me to make it good."

"So I did." I leaned back in my chair, arms folding over my chest. "Fuck me, Jake. At least tell me she's pretty."

"He was. She's not."

"Jesus—"

Jake's laughter filled the office. Before he returned to his own desk, I'd shredded the paper, returning to the investigation Ethan had outlined.

The cattle rustlers hadn't been found, though it was only a matter of time before they were tracked. Buying Kinland Creek cattle would be high on a lot of lists, but they were also memorable stock, and with the news story going out tonight, there was a high chance they'd be found.

The local police department had been very forgiving of my stepping into their jurisdiction, though I suspected they wouldn't have been half as kind if my boss hadn't offered a joint training day for the local precinct.

Henderson wasn't saying a word to us, but Ethan had his favorite hard-ass look on when he headed into the interrogation room. I wanted to be a fly on the wall in that conversation, but there was someone who needed me more.

Maybe I just needed her.

Placing my feet carefully on her wooden floorboards, I remembered how noisy they'd been last time I was in her house. Not a window was open, though the door hadn't been latched. Worry gnawed at the pit of my stomach.

Light from the street lamps that lined the road at the front of her house reflected along the hallway. I reached the end, checking each room as I went, though I hadn't found Ella's bedroom yet. The place seemed vacant.

Every shadow flickered, shifting in the early evening light, and each was a threat with my exhausted senses on hyper-alert.

I checked the back door, but at least that was locked. The last room was off the back of her living room.

With no sign of anyone around, I cursed myself for not calling someone to watch her house. If the rustlers had been good mates with Henderson, they might hunt her for revenge. Had he called my name in, or hers? She'd seen them, could identify them.

Damnit.

I really didn't have my head screwed on straight. Staring across to the final doorway that had to be her room, I paused. The door was open.

I hovered inside the doorway, checking either side of me, but there was no movement in the deep shadow of the room. I lowered my gun and took a cautious step inside.

All hell broke loose.

Ella shot upright in her bed, flailing covers and sheets like an apparition on speed, her scream choked by a strangled

201

moan of pain. I called out, but even in the dark, I could see that she couldn't recognize me.

"Ella." I took a step forward; she screamed louder, clutching her side. So much for suburban bliss. I flicked the light switch on. Whimpering, she covered her eyes, still tangled in sheets.

"Let me help you," I said softly.

Ella stopped screaming, and blinked. Her rose-pink mouth half agape, she stared up at me from beneath a tangle of blankets and mussed hair.

I grinned at the sight of her. Even mussed and half terrified, the woman she had grown into was sexy as all hell.

Her eyes narrowed as the situation dawned on her. Ella harrumphed, flinging the covers back. A flash of curved calf and bare feet slipped from beneath the sheets.

My mouth dried, tracing her pale skin to the hem of her lacy and very translucent nightgown.

"You are an asshole, Andy Matthews," she grumped.

I plopped on her bed by her feet, lifting them over my lap. My fingers traced patterns over her skin.

202

She leaned back on an enormous pile of pillows that half propped her up with a soft sigh of pleasure.

That will be the first of many, if I have my way.

"I've been called worse." I nodded to the pillows. "Comfy?"

"Bet your ass."

"It's the drugs." It dawned on me; my God, I needed to clear my head space. "That's why you're swearing." And I'd left the door open. *Idiot.* "I'll be right back."

Mentally slapping myself, I latched the front door and returned to my spot, sliding a little higher along her legs. My fingers trailed along the inside of her knee, and she sighed.

"Your door was open. I thought—" My breath caught as my imagined scenarios ran through my head — what had happened to her, what I might find.

"Oh." Ella considered for a moment. "Did you talk to your boss?"

"No beating around the bush with you like this, is there?"

"Nope."

"Yeah, I spoke to Ethan. Or rather, he spoke to me. They– they want to give me some award. I've knocked it back," I warned her as she lit up, a giant grin spreading over her face.

She settled back on the pillows, a smug smile gracing her beautiful face. "So...you're still a Ranger."

"Yes, ma'am. Do you still think you're not worthy of being the wife of one?"

"What?"

I inhaled a sharp breath and held it for a second, my heart racing. The thought had been running about in my head the entire time I'd been apart from her. Ducking home when I'd arrived back in Austin, I'd grabbed a fresh shirt and dug through my gun safe, but I knew it was still there in the tiny box at the top, unopened.

"You said you couldn't stay with me because you weren't high enough up the social ladder, that you'd damage my career. But it would never have impacted my future, because that future was you. I'll make my way on honest, damned hard work on my own, if that sort of thing ever comes into play."

Ella watched me with wide eyes, gripping her bed covers with whitening knuckles.

I dug into my pocket and extracted the box, turning it over in my hands.

"I know it would have been a big ask, back then. I'd just graduated, and you were still in school. But we're ten years older and...we both know who we are, now. So, Ella Harding," I flipped the lid open on the solitaire diamond I'd purchased so many years ago and had kept in the hope I might need it again, one day. "Will you marry a Ranger?"

Her eyes bright, Ella blinked a few times. The same glow she'd had after we'd made love spread over her, and I knew her answer before she said it.

Though it must have hurt like hell, Ella leaned forward, sliding her arms around my shoulders, and kissed me. My heart swelled. Holding tight, she kissed me as though she never wanted to let go. I swore I never would.

"Yes, Andy. I would love to marry you."

I slipped the ring over her finger. It went over the knuckle with little resistance. She really hadn't changed that much in ten years, and everything that had changed was still amazing to me.

I kissed her again, leaning her back into the mountain of pillows, and began to

figure out how to free her from her
nightgown.

If you loved Andy and Ella,
follow Jake into the next Texan Devils story:

www.books2read.com/TD2

Jake Masters is the sassy contingent of his Texas Ranger unit with a penchant for baristas—of either the male or female variety. If his smart mouth isn't getting him in trouble, his indiscretions on his boss's desk are.

When his complicated relationship and flings converge, Jake takes the assignment his boss offers with a strong dose of relief—investigate a human trafficking ring that crosses international borders. The case proves more difficult than he expected, but a little tough love from his home office tells Jake that he's handling this investigation alone.

A local barista provides an excellent distraction from his woes. Jake discovers that his new crush is entangled with the trafficked women. Before he can give her his heart, he has to work out which side she's on.

ACKNOWLEDGEMENTS

Working on a brand new book, or a brand new series is always amazing. A whole cast of new characters, a whole new world to look at, especially when I'm looking at it from the other side of the world. First and foremost, thank you Courtney for giving me insight into Texas and a new place to love and all things Texas Rangers. And Jacinta for supporting my Chuck Norris obsession over the years and sparking my Texas Rangers passion to a whole new level. I'm grateful, truely.

None of my characters would be the same without the eyes of my amazing critique partners, Jo Creed and Samantha Adair. You girls bring the heartstrings every time!

Ashley Strom works her butt off removing all my Aussie slang and replacing them with appropriate cussing, plus polishing my stories until they shine. It's a massive learning curve and I desperately want to visit all the places now!

My betas and ARC readers — you guys seriously rock. You rise to the challenge each time without fail and I'm so blessed to be surrounded by such an enthusiastic and loyal team.

209

A book isn't pretty until you have the right cover art. JS Designs have worked tirelessly to create Red Hart Ranch's sprawling landscape and logo. I could stare at that all day!

But a story isn't a book without its readers. Thankyou for reading all the way to the finish, and I truly hope you enjoyed Ella and Andy's Christmas. There are many more to come.

Sofia xx

About the Author

Sofia Aves writes fast-paced police romances, suspenseful mysteries, steamy cowboys with a Montana backdrop and the occasional cheeky god. She loves reading Indie authors and hides her collection of college romance books beneath an ever-growing TBR pile.

Sofia is a mum of three crazies and an overly large fur baby who thinks she's a teacup puppy. She loves orchids but can't always keep them alive. Sofia lives near Brisbane, Australia.

www.sofiaves.com

Join Sofia's newsletter & get a free Blue Blooded Brothers short story:
https://BookHip.com/CNMQFX

Follow Sofia on BookBub:
https://www.bookbub.com/profile/sofia-aves?follw=true

MORE BY SOFIA AVES

BLUE BLOODED BROTHERS SERIES

Recommended reading order

213

COWBOYS & WESTERNS

RED HART RANCH

SNOW ON THE RANGE

SIREN ON THE RANGE

SUNDOWN ON THE RANGE

TEXAN DEVILS

RANGER'S WISH

RANGER BEDEVILLED

RANGER'S DESIRE

PARANORMAL ROMANCE

<u>TRICKSTER'S LAW</u>

<u>A PORTRAIT IN ASH AND LACE</u>

*Read on for the first chapter of
Cal and Mila's story in*

COLLISION
Blue Blooded Brothers book 1...

CHAPTER ONE

MILA

Tiny feet pattered the worn carpet, glitter coating it with false splendour. The little girl wended her way between patrons. Some were blessed with stars, some with promises of happiness and love; others became apples and bananas. Too much *Ben and Holly*, I recalled from when I'd been forced to babysit for my best friend.

I tried not to look over to my left, the red shoe that– I spun away, and refocused on my task. The man behind me shuffled his feet. I flinched as he dug the pistol into the small of my back, and shivered, my skin prickling.

The small office of Central Bank was being held up, and no one outside had noticed. Business operated as usual in the main street through the broad, glassed front as it did every day.

"Oooh, sweetheart, you cold there? I'll warm you up." Foetid breath beneath a rough growl assailed me. I repressed the urge to turn away or vomit, knowing it would only provoke him further. Clammy warmth rubbed my side. My stomach clenched, fighting the numbness that spread through me until I was ice.

A beep sounded at my last keystroke. It was a welcome distraction from my self-analysis. As the thug moved away, I squinted at a screen I'd never seen before.

"It's asking for a password." My voice was husky from lack of use, or maybe it was from screaming silently inside.

"What? No, ...Oi! Nerd! You never said nothin' 'bout no flamin' password!"

Black wire glasses appeared above the divider between the teller cubes. A tuft of dark hair wobbled above a brow furrowed in concentration.

"Seriously, already? Hang on, how far has she got?" Glasses grimaced at me theatrically from his seat at the opposite counter, rolling eyes in the direction of the stale-breathed thug. I returned the sentiment, if only mentally. There was no way I wanted any of these aggressors believing I sympathized with them.

"I'm as far as the login for the manager's screen," I snapped, short breaths puffing through a clenched chest.

Get it over, quick and easy; then they'll be gone.

218

It was the mantra that had been running through my head for the past twenty minutes.

Get it over, over.

Behind the partition, another patron was being turned into a banana.

We thought we'd been well prepared for an armed robbery. The thin booklet on personal safety was required reading. Give them what they want, and they will leave. Sound the silent alarm behind your terminal.

Karen had tried to do that.

I refused to look at her desk again, my stomach heaving. HR's strategy hadn't worked this time. Maybe I should send them a memo on it, come Monday.

If I was still breathing, then.

"Only the login? That's disappointing." Glasses' brow furrowed deeply. "She should have passed that, already. I gave you the codes for those, before...well," he waved a hand behind himself, where a body lay: Karen — the teller who had manned the desk where Glasses now sat before she was yanked from the line of hostages. A swell of emotion blurred my eyes. I blinked tears away angrily.

Don't think, don't think. Over. Get it over and done.

Focus.

Tapped the keyboard, wiggled the mouse. Breathe.

Don't engage. Don't.

"Passwords?"

I was proud my voice didn't shake. My logical brain informed me it was shock and nothing that was under my control. The emotional part didn't answer; it was as numb as the rest of me.

Glasses raised his eyebrows.

"Yes, ma'am."

He flicked a brief salute. A scrap of paper fluttered from his fingers, landing beside the keyboard.

"*Fluffy22?* Really?" I couldn't help commenting. "Cat or dog?"

"Likely the goldfish. Some people have no idea, truly," Glasses responded with a roll of his eyes. We shared a look. I realized what I was doing and quickly returned to the screen: Staring, willing tunnel vision.

Don't, don't.

Heavy footsteps reverberated behind me where the bank manager's office sat. A heavy hand clapped down on my shoulder. Too hot, too overly familiar. His thumb rubbed the sensitive spot on my collarbone, forcing an unwelcome shiver through me.

I willed myself still, to not react, desperate to return to the blank nothing that had consumed me only a moment before, though the urge to jerk away lingered when he spoke. Deep and cold. The same voice I had heard beside Karen.

Before.

"How're we going, we in yet?"

"Not yet, boss; gotta put these in," Glasses indicated the passwords, "Then we should have full access."

I still couldn't believe it. These guys were going to bungle their own robbery. My screen had no way to access the electronic locks for the safe, and anyway, it was such a small branch. Surely, nothing they held would be sufficient to risk years of incarceration. Reflex had my mouth open to say as much until my brain kicked into gear. My mouth closed with a snap. The three men turned to look at me, and I started guiltily.

"Something you'd like to add, lass?" The question was delivered with some small humour and a touch of annoyance. I shook my head mutely.

"Right, let's get this show on the road."

I chanced a glimpse up at the man behind the robbery: tanned skin, longer-than-average dark hair, hard jaw. Tall and lean. You were supposed to remember details like that for the police, right? His face swiveled my way, displaying ice-cold eyes, unsuited to the rest of his handsome frame.

The devil within, I thought numbly. That wasn't a face that would be easy to forget. I'd have no trouble describing him later, I knew. With hands beginning to tremor from the proximity of the man responsible for the death of my friend, I entered the passwords as the prompts came up. A tiny box popped up in the center of the screen that I had never seen before.

"...And we're in." Glasses leaned over the divider, meerkat style. "Thanks, love." He winked at me, tapping furiously on a portable keyboard he'd rolled out on the desktop. "Ta-daa."

With a dramatic flourish over his head and the tap of a final keystroke, my screen winked, flickered to blue, and reopened. The little cursor moved around with a mind of its own, opening areas,

222

changing settings. Glasses was manipulating my computer remotely.

More tapping, a little head bobbing, and a clunk came from the rear of the office space — *the safe*. The lights flickered briefly, and I looked around. The three men moved away in a synchronized motion that made me wonder if they'd practiced it. Suddenly left alone and grateful for it, I exhaled a long breath that left me more empty than before. One of the men sauntered back out, standing beside the last person in the row of hostages.

Every one of them tensed, and I wondered if they were thinking of the same sound as I did as it ricocheted around my head. Clangs and swearing came from the rear of the bank. I realised I knew less about the bank I'd worked in for three years than I had thought.

Distracted by a swirl of glitter, I looked over at the rows of patrons lining the wall opposite my station: the little girl tracing invisible pictures on the neutral carpet with a sparkling princess wand; a lone, glossy, red shoe, involuntarily discarded upon impact. A stockinged foot, partly visible, protruding behind a cubicle. I dragged my gaze away.

Sit still. Don't think. Don't.

A shadow flitted across the windows that looked out onto the street from the front of the small bank. From their positions on the floor pressed against the wall opposite the teller stations, customers — hostages — shifted uncomfortably, attempting to appear insignificant. Up top, I was exposed, the downlights above me driving sweat around my collar, though it ran down my back cold. I wasn't sure if it was fuelled by fear or heat.

My water bottle cooled my palms, and I slugged down water like a thirsty camel, placing it back on the desk. I shuffled pencils in their holder, ordering them neatly by height. It gave my hands something to do. I took a long, deep breath and tried to settle, to be calm. Letting my eyes close out the rest of the office, I focused on my breath, trying to ignore the sounds behind me. It took a few tries, but I almost had it down, the panic beginning to recede, until I remembered that Karen was the one who had taught me the technique.

My heart pounded anew as I tried to erase the image. Numb fingers fumbled my water bottle, slipping on the condensation coating the clear plastic. It spun in the air, too fast for water to escape, though its movement seemed slow enough to me.

I almost had one hand — who was I kidding; it was the tip of my finger — on the bottle when a loud clang startled me. I fumbled the bottle a second time, wide-eyed as it hit the floor, emptying its contents. I jerked as a small, black wooden box appeared in the corner of my vision and slid forward.

Tanned hands attached to thick forearms reached across my desk. I would have loved them if I hadn't known who they belonged to. I was a sucker for well-muscled forearms, but not at this moment. Fine, white linen sleeves, rolled to the elbows, looked so out of place — an involuntary glance once again gave the impression of a wealthy businessman, not a bank robber.

Murderer.

Gaze fixed, he cradled the box, caressed the lid. It was such an intimate gesture; it felt as though I was intruding on a personal moment. I inched away discreetly until the edge of my chair bit into the backs of my thighs.

Fear permeated the thickened air — from me, and the gallery on the floor. The man behind the robbery stared at the dark, little box with greedy eyes. Glasses appeared, hovering in my peripheral vision.

He annoyed me, and I wanted to bat him away. A twitch in the robber's shoulder left me thinking he felt the same.

Stop sympathising with them.

Reluctantly, one tanned hand released its prize, extended in a beseeching gesture. A tiny tremor quaked through the limb. With no small amount of ceremony, Glasses produced a minuscule key, placing it into the hollow cup of his upturned palm.

The little, silver scrap glinted dully — antique-looking — until the tip. I squinted and leaned forward, trying to discern the markings at the bottom of the filigree blade. The end curled upward, screwlike. The inserted key would have to be twisted or wound, like an old music box.

Reverently, the key was lowered to the lock, almost touching. Silence reigned; within the little cluster, no breath escaped.

The moment shattered abruptly, along with the glass of the large, street-front window. A dark shadow blasted through, into the foyer of the bank, showering everyone in glittering shards. Scarlet and indigo lights reflected in the glass littering the carpet. Voices cried out — a high, thin shriek piercing above the rest.

"Daddy!" A little sob accompanied the cry. The group surrounding me broke up, the small, black box forgotten in a surge of movement. The two men who had held the hostages at bay accompanied their leader toward the mess of glass, weapons fluidly drawn as one.

These men have worked together before.

I studied the changed scene before me as though I were the one behind glass; a shiny, black Jeep protruded into the cavity that used to be the front of the bank. Blue and red lights hung slightly lopsided, the odd flash blinding and disappearing in a staccato motion, adding to the surreality of the image.

Lots of extra attachments I was sure wouldn't be on a regular, stock model hung from the vehicle. A loud whoop came from within the open-topped cab, the flashing lights turned off, and everyone in the bank froze.

Two heads emerged from behind the black utility dash. One, a shag of blonde hair bearing a cheeky grin out of place in the sombre atmosphere. The other, a weather-worn face, covered in a beard that looked

227

more suited to a motorcycle gang. He bore a resigned expression.

The shaggy-haired driver hoisted himself onto his seat in full view of the three men, who aimed their guns at him. His mouth moved, some throwaway line I missed. *What a cowboy*. The thieves evidently agreed; from my view of their backs as they moved forward, their leader shook his head, his fine shirt barely creasing with effort as he raised his weapon.

"Hold on there, John Wayne," he drawled with a tinge of sarcasm, "this here's my bank."

Shaggy gave a cocky, lopsided grin. "I've always fancied myself more as Wyatt Earp. At least he could shoot."

He held out a hand — rather pompously, I thought — and the man still seated in the passenger seat of the Jeep tossed him a long firearm. No expert on guns, I watched the exchange with fascination.

"Oh, let him have his small moment of glory."

Shaggy drew and aimed, managing to pose at the same time. I fought the urge to roll my eyes, unable to feel the fear I knew I should — entranced by the drama unfolding before me. Shaggy's firearm was matte black, matching the Jeep. Clean and pristine.

"And I half expected it to be a six-shooter." The dark man tilted his head briefly to the side. "Step aside, now. Your time in the limelight is over." A sideways glance to his team, speaking just loud enough that I could hear him, "It's time to go."

"Hold it, gents!" Shaggy seemed surprised he had lost control over the situation — if he'd ever had it. His partner started to stand also, groping the bench seat behind him when a sharp report broke the unreality of their playacting. The hostages ducked in a wave as the man to the left of the posse's leader fired a single shot.

Shaggy's partner disappeared beneath the dash. The young cop attempted to do the same, but seemed to slip, teetering comically sideways for a moment before toppling over the back of the driver's seat with a short yell. There was a thump as he landed. The moment the cop was down, the three men in front lowered their weapons, advancing towards the newly-created exit in unison.

Glasses scurried up, collected the key with a quick wink, and followed the team outside, flanked by the man with bad breath. A white transit van drew up to the curb, and the men disappeared inside.

The van moved off. I sat, frozen completely, unable to process the situation. Sirens approached from the opposite direction. Lights lit up the bank interior like Christmas, reflecting off broken glass scattered on the floor in a kaleidoscope of colour.

Reversing, the Jeep disappeared back through the hole it had created in the bank's only window, following the direction the white van had taken. Emergency vehicles rushed past in a string of flashing lights.

It's like something out of a movie.

Dazed hostages paused, watching. Glances were exchanged, though no one spoke. Fear and uncertainty still hung in the air. After a moment, the spell was broken, and movement resumed. Customers stirred, no longer cowering beneath armed aggressors. Soft chatter filled the ruined bank.

I knew I should ask them to sit alone, quietly, so their stories wouldn't be confused by each other's interpretations of what they had just endured. My training kicked in, my brain screaming at me to move, but I couldn't.

Glass tinkled as it was brushed from clothing. Swivelling slightly, I made to stand. On the desk behind me, stood the wooden box. Wouldn't the thieves be furious when they realised Glasses had taken the key but forgotten the box? One of the patrons who had been cowering against my counter leaned over to me.

"Looks like they left something important behind," he said with a sad smile. I nodded, still staring at the box, lost in thought. A tiny sob broke the murmur from the hostages, and we both looked up.

The little girl stood in the centre of the wreckage, her glitter wand drooping to brush the faded carpet, covered with a different sort of sparkle.

Eyes wide, I turned to the man who had spoken, recognising him as the owner of a local grocery store.

"I think they left behind more than one thing."

Silence fell, heavy as a shroud. Heads turned to the little girl who wandered aimlessly in the centre of the deconstructed bank, tears coursing down a face partially covered by dirty-blonde locks. Dust motes danced around the small figure in the afternoon light as brightly decorated police cars drew up along the bank front. Men swarmed toward the window.

The wand dropped to the floor.

"Daddy?"

Read Cal and Mila's story here:
www.books2read.com/Collision-LQP

POLITICS AND PAPERWORK

A Blue Blooded Brothers Novella

Liam is constantly swamped beneath the politics of managing an elite task force. Now, given more downtime than he can handle, the ex-special ops sniper flounders to find purpose outside the strict rigours of his working day.

Selena has been Liam's best friend for nearly fifteen years. Elegant and intelligent, and a partner in her own law firm, she's helped Liam through difficult cases, as well as the aftermath of PTSD. Watching Liam drown in day-to-day life, Selena ups the stakes with a little flirting to restore life to the man she adores.

When a series of vandalisms target Selena, Liam is determined to keep the captivating solicitor safe, so long as she lets him. Intent on playing her game by his own rules, Liam risks an uncertain future for the woman he's always loved.

Liam and Selena's story will continue in RECKONING.

www.books2read.com/politicsandpaperwork

BLINDSIDED

As the youngest member of an elite task force team and built as big as they come, Danny is often underestimated. It's an image he encourages, despite sporting a genius level IQ. Currently screwing his boss' ex and with a big problem for authority, Danny is sent to professional development coaching. He hates the idea – he's got determination in spades to do what it takes in his job and personal life, and thrashes against it until he meets Laura, the sexy motivator who shows him he is worth more than what he believes. When the team begins working Operation Predator, Danny's moment of peace is shot to hell.

Danny is sent to professional coaching as part of his boss, Cal's, efforts to hold the team together after their last operation. When he discovers his motivator is the gorgeous jogger he's been working out with, Danny is determined to flirt his way through his coaching, stubbornly refusing to delve into personal truths he's been hiding from himself for years. He's relieved when he's placed on an undercover assignment – his preferred area of expertise.

Moving in with a group of gym junkies isn't a bad way to spend assignment – especially when he gets to hack as well. The group remove small change from banks, but Danny feels there is something bigger in the works – until he is spotted by Laura, who almost blows his cover. Pulled from his assignment, Danny is furious. Tensions rise during their coaching sessions as more odd hacks catch Danny's attention.

Their budding relationship is blown to pieces when he opts to go back undercover, determined not to let Laura distract him.

www.books2read.com/Blindsided-BBB2

TRICKSTER'S LAW

A child isn't born evil...is he?

Mischief-maker, silver tongue, trickster... Mayhem follows Loki throughout the nine realms, earning him a reputation as a bringer of chaos. But there is more to Loki than mortals see, and life is boring for an immortal when no one really *gets him*.

A little mischief is harmless in the hands of a god, right?

Companion to Odin and Thor but shunned by the Norse gods of the Æsir, Loki still seeks their acceptance. No matter how many times he saves their supreme backsides, his every effort ends with a death threat casually tossed in his direction.

Increasing his attempts to impress the Æsir, Loki tires of their constant disdain despite his successes in their impossible challenges. So, he turns to what he does best: chaos.

Follow the trickster god Loki through the perfectly normal life of a disillusioned god, and find out what makes him NOT SO...EVIL.

This is a standalone novel in a collaboration of origin stories.
www.books2read.com/TrickstersLaw

CPSIA information can be obtained
at www.ICGtesting.com
Printed in the USA
LVHW041533191121
703843LV00021B/1978